BHUPEN KHAKHAR

BHUPEN KHAKHAR

MAGANBHAI'S GLUE, PAGES FROM A DIARY, VADKI, PHOREN SOAP AND MAUJILA MANILAL

translated by

GANESH DEVY, NAUSHIL MEHTA AND BINA SRINIVASAN

First published by Katha in 2001

KATHA
A-3 Sarvodaya Enclave
Sri Aurobindo Marg
New Delhi 110 017
Phone: 652 4350, 652 4511
Fax: 651 4373
E-mail: kathavilasam@katha.org
Internet address: http://www.katha.org

KATHA is a registered nonprofit society devoted to enhancing the pleasures of reading. KATHA VILASAM is its story research and resource centre.

Cover and inside illustrations: Bhupen Khakhar
Cover Design: Geeta Dharmarajan
In-house editors: Gita Rajan, Shoma Choudhury

Typeset in 9 on 15.5pt Bookman by Suresh Sharma
at Katha and Printed at Pauls Press, New Delhi

ISBN 81-87649-12-7

2 4 6 8 10 9 7 5 3 1

CONTENTS

MAGANBHAI'S GLUE

One day I was on the way to my office in Makarpura Industrial Estate when a dark complexioned dhoti kurta clad stranger waved out to me near Bhavan's School. I stopped my scooter.

He said, You work at Shah & Co in C-3. My factory is in C-12. Right across your office. Can you give me a lift? From there I have to go to the bank for some urgent work.

Without waiting for an answer, he settled down on the pillion seat with both his legs on one side. His khadi dhoti fluttered like a flag in the wind. Soon we reached C-12. He stepped down, shook my hand and said, I'm Maganbhai Pathak. That's my little factory. Do come over some time. Thanks for the ride.

By the time I parked the scooter, he had disappeared.

I thought of Maganbhai a few days later. During my lunch break, I went over to C-12, a shed of corrugated metal sheets. Maganbhai sat on a stool stirring an iron rod in a large vessel heated by a kerosene stove. The stove was noisy, so he motioned me to the only other piece of furniture in the shed – a wooden chair – and pushed a pack of beedis and a matchbox towards me. I lit a beedi.

There was a heap of grey powder in one corner of the shed. Two, three jute bags lay on it. A couple of shirts hung from nails on the walls. It wasn't easy to sit near the hot stove with the afternoon sun beating down on the metal roof.

I stepped out to smoke my beedi. I was taking the last drag when Maganbhai came out and said, Do come in. I've put off the stove.

As I went in, I asked, What's the grey powder used for?

It's aluminium powder, he replied enthusiastically. He extracted a chemistry book from his shoulder bag and tried to explain to me how it was manufactured. I couldn't make any sense of the chemical formulae so he explained, This powder is used in firecrackers. When you light sparklers, the bright white sparks are due to the aluminium powder.

Are you going to dispatch this powder to Sivakasi?

I'm going to sell it to firecracker manufacturers right here in Vadodara. There's a good profit margin in this line.

Have you hired a salesman?

Maganbhai didn't reply but turned some pages of his chemistry book.

It was clear to me that Maganbhai had not studied more than four years of English in school – if that. I was impressed by the fact that he could read an English text as dense as this and put it to profitable use.

I was about to get up and leave when someone entered the shed. Maganbhai made the introductions, This is my partner Bhagirath Patel, and then, pointing a finger at me, He handles the accounts in the office across the street.

We exchanged greetings. I vacated the wooden chair for Bhagirathbhai and returned to my office.

Months later, one winter evening, Maganbhai entered my office at five thirty wearing a beige coat over white dhoti kurta.

I greeted him. Welcome, Maganbhai! I've been busy the last few months. We accountants get busy after Diwali. Accounts are audited every January so we have to be prepared. But tell me, how are you? How's your aluminium powder business?

Maganbhai's reply was strange. What can I say? I've been so busy for the last three months ... Look here. I need to talk to you. I'll come with you to your place today and you must drop me home at night. Got that?

He gave me no choice. I wondered who gave him the right to make decisions for me.

Fifteen minutes later, I had wound up my work at the office and we were riding my scooter.

I picked up milk, sugar, ganthia and chivda from Shiv Traders on the way home.

It was six thirty by the time we negotiated the city traffic and reached home. Winter darkness greeted us. I opened the door, switched on the lights, made some tea and served the snacks.

Maganbhai picked up a handful of chivda as he said, I stopped making aluminium powder two months ago. There's no future in that line. My partner Bhagirath doesn't want to invest any more money. So I've parted with him and rented another place in the Estate – in C-25.

With that, he extracted the frayed chemistry book from his shoulder bag. An ornate wedding invitation served as a bookmark. He opened the book on the marked page and offered it to me. Squiggles of chemical formulae communicated nothing to me.

Maganbhai realized this and said, See. This is the procedure for making a new kind of glue. Everyone makes glue according to the first three formulae. What sells in the market today is glue made from only the first three formulae. I'm going to make glue according to Formula Number Four.

I could make nothing of the two line formula so I offered him some more chivda.

Maganbhai took another handful of it and said, This glue is so strong that if a drop spills on the floor and your finger touches that spot ... either your finger has to be cut off or the tile removed from the floor. Then you have to live with the tile stuck to your finger for the rest of your life. Look here. Two, three cases are described here ... A man once sat down on the floor where this glue had spilled. Despite all efforts he could not be separated from the floor. Finally he went to a doctor with the two tiles still stuck to his bottom. The tiles were separated after surgery ... Did you know that Siamese twins exhibited in circuses are actually stuck together with this glue. It's available only in a remote city of Guyana ... It's difficult to make and even more difficult to preserve ... I've spent a lot of money to build special vessels ... Just you see! When this glue is made, we'll be able to take two elephants and stick them together ... It'll be easy to construct buildings! Just build an entire floor on the ground, apply this glue on its bottom, pick up the whole structure with a crane and place it on the building! It'll no longer be necessary to build a scaffolding to construct a ten, fifteen storey building.

I suggested, All this will cost a lot of money.

But Maganbhai replied confidently, I've applied for a loan from a bank and my new partner is interested in this glue. Saheb, it's just a matter of two years. There will be no substitute for this glue in the world! Just imagine! What will join railway compartments? My glue! What will you need to join three aeroplanes and fly them together? My glue! What will you need to build the body of a motorcar? Just apply my glue below the body and place it on the engine! No need for welding!

I tried to add a practical note to the conversation, How long before the loan is passed?

Ten days at the most. Bhagatbhai knows someone in the bank. He's going to look after the entire distribution of my glue. We've received applications from ten, twenty salesmen. Everything will soon be finalized. Then we'll be flooded with riches!

Maganbhai went on praising his glue as he sat eating ganthia and chivda. I too started thinking enthusiastically about his business.

Late at night, Maganbhai said, It's too late to go home now. I'll stay the night here.

I went with my tiffin box to buy dinner. When I returned, Maganbhai was fast asleep on my bed. His eyes reminded me of the long eyed Tirthankar idols. How could I wake him up?

I had my dinner and slept on the floor that night.

About ten days later I went over to meet Maganbhai. He was not in his new office. One man, presumably Bhagatbhai, his new partner, sat stirring a liquid with an iron rod.

I introduced myself and asked, Where's Maganbhai?

Bhagatbhai shrugged and said, I don't know. Last week he went off with Khandwawala Toofani Baba.

When will he be back?

No one knows. His wife said that whenever Khandwawala Baba shouts out his name from the street, Maganbhai goes off with him without even bothering to change his clothes. No one can tell when he'll be back.

Tell me, how's business?

Just started. The Formula is still to be fully decoded. When Maganbhai returns, we'll begin production.

I returned to my office and my ledgers.

A week later, Maganbhai came to my office at five thirty in the evening wearing the same beige coat. Once again we bought ganthia and chivda on the way. We reached my house and I made tea. Maganbhai made himself comfortable on my blue bedspread.

I asked, Where were you? When I went to your office, Bhagatbhai was stirring glue in the vessel.

Maganbhai spoke as if he had not heard me, Khandwawala Baba had come. He called out for me and said, Come with me at once! I just had time to put on my chappals. No time to take any money with me ... I've known him for years. He stays in a little room at Surpaneshwar Ashram. Those who feel like it come and give him food. He stays there all by himself for six months a year. Doesn't mingle with other residents of the ashram. If anyone asks him questions about sansara he hurls insults at them. So people are afraid of asking him anything ... He lands up in Vadodara every once in a while. He stands on the street near my house and calls out my name ... I go with him to Karjan, Undera, Nareshwar. I listen to whatever he says to people. This time I was with him for a week. When I returned, I didn't even have the rail fare. But he put me on a train. I travelled without a ticket to Vadodara.

How did you meet him?

When I visited Surpanashewar Ashram years ago, I heard that a Khandwawala Baba lived there. I went to seek his darshan and saw that he never said a useless word. If anyone dared to ask what should one do to find God, he'd hurl an insult at him and say, Go buy a matchbox and set fire to your sansara! Then come back to me with your desire to find God! Upon hearing such acidic pronouncements, I felt a deep respect towards him and became his devotee.

He then told me about the Baba's teachings, Nabhishwas, Sushnamala, Ida and Pingla Nadi, the yoga breathing techniques. We talked till late that night.

I thought of Maganbhai often but it had become difficult to meet him. He would be busy meeting a chemistry professor at the university about the Formula Number Four glue. The professor had telephoned Delhi and finally London about Maganbhai's queries.

One evening, when I went to meet Maganbhai, Bhagatbhai was stirring the iron rod in the vessel containing Formula Two glue. He looked as though he was cooking doodhpak. His smile had dried up.

Bhagatbhai declared, See, I told Maganbhai, It's okay if we can't make Number Four glue. Let's make Number Two glue so we can get our money back! But Khandwawala Baba has pronounced that Number Four glue will surely be made one day. Only we'll have to work hard. So Maganbhai goes and spends all day pursuing chemistry professors!

I sensed his impatience as he poured the Number Two glue carefully into small blue plastic bottles arranged in neat rows. As soon as the glue cooled, he would stir the vessel as if it was a pot of doodhpak.

After watching him for a while, I left for home.

Two weeks later, one afternoon Maganbhai came to my office dressed shabbily. He had a three day stubble. His hands were unwashed. Before I could greet him, he announced, Saheb! The formula is ready! Calling up the laboratory in London solved the last factor. The product will be ready in three, four days!

Before I could respond, he began walking away.

I wanted to know a lot more. I persuaded him to meet me that evening. But when I went to pick him up, his factory was locked.

Six days passed. We did not meet. I couldn't hold myself back any longer. I went over to his office. It was in complete chaos. Bhagatbhai's hand was stuck to the vessel, a worker's bottom was stuck to a plate, many floor tiles had come off, an office folder had frozen in the vessel, hardened paper balls were stuck all over the place, spilled glue had frozen into milky little hills all over the floor. There were a few foot high hills in the middle of the shed. A woman wearing a red sari stood with her hand stuck to the switchboard.

When I looked down from the window, I could see three people stuck in different poses to the handle, the mudguard and the seat of a bicycle. It was a scene straight out of a Marx Brothers' film.

As I climbed down the staircase, I saw a dishevelled Maganbhai rushing in with two doctors. He didn't notice me.

When I went to meet him a month later, the entire scene had changed. About ten women sat on the floor with chaklas and belans – rolling what looked like pooris. Mountains of small balls of dough were neatly arranged on large copper plates. Maganbhai sat there handing out the balls of dough to the women. He was surprised to see me. He greeted me as if we were meeting after years, Hello, Mr Accountant! Haven't seen you for a while! Found time after ages, have you? Looks like you've forgotten me!

His voice was joyous. He looked quite different from the dishevelled Maganbhai who had brought the doctors. Today, in his impeccably bordered khadi dhoti, kurta and sleeveless jacket, he could barely contain his excitement.

He sent for tea. He poured half the tea into the saucer, offered the cup to me and slurped from the saucer.

As I sat sipping the tea in my cup, Maganbhai confessed, The Number Four glue was a nightmare. The entire staff – everyone – got stuck. I was away with Khandwawala Baba. When I returned I saw this drama. I went and got some doctors. Everyone was admitted to the hospital. But Saheb! What a glue it was, that Formula Number Four! With one drop you could have stuck two elephants together! But Bhagatbhai threw up his hands ... He would not speak a word to me after returning from the hospital ... Sold off all the vessels at the factory. Returned the bank loan. Tore up the partnership deeds. He was about to walk out when he saw my chemistry book. He picked it up and tore each page into four pieces and lit a bonfire of all the five hundred pages before he left ... I've not seen him since.

I could not resist asking, When did you start this new business?

Bhagatbhai had burnt my business dictionary ... I was wondering what to do next when Devdatt, my cousin, came over to meet me. He suggested, Maganbhai! There's a great demand for Indian snacks in America. Why don't you make something that can be exported there? I'll finance such a business!

Then?

For the next three days I looked for items to export. I prepared a long list. I was looking for edible items that won't spoil for weeks. I thought of pickles – Mango, Limo, Black Pepper, Green Pepper, Gunda, Garmar, Gol-keri, Chhundo, and Murabbo. To get the recipes right, I bought five books including *Chaalo Rasodama* and *Rasmadhuri*. But Devdatt crumpled my list, threw it away and said, Ten, twelve companies export pickles like these. No one will buy our pickles! All my efforts ended up into the wastepaper basket along with my crushed lists. The next two days, long lists of traditional recipes whirled around my head like throbbing headaches. Sometimes a list of sour, fermented items like dhokla would occupy my mind and at other times I would want to take off to California with Devdatt, set up shop there and sell piping hot pakodas, fulvadis and kachoris ... Those times I'd need to drink a masala soda to squash such longings. Finally, it came down to papads. Devdatt called them Pappadoms like Americans. But we moved from the idea of making pappadoms to khakhras – and finally to small khakhras – as snacks to accompany drinks. Devdatt loved the idea of mini khakhras. The next day we became partners. I invested my efforts and Devdatt his cash. He gave me five thousand dollars and returned to America. I created this world of mini khakhras from his dollars.

True to his nature, Maganbhai now became a khakhra enthusiast. Expert advice flowed from him on this subject.

To the two women who sat holding pieces of white cotton towels to pan roast fifteen small khakhras, he said, Look here! These khakhras are not destined for India! They're on their way to America! Where? America! We have to fly the flag of our fame over there! Understood? They like everything clean there! Not like this! Pieces of white cotton towels lying on the floor ... Huh! What's that?

The women said, A brass plate that was washed thoroughly with water and dried.

Maganbhai hovered about excitedly.

When I got up to leave, he asked, Shall I come over this evening?

I've to go over to a friend's place for dinner.

Oh yes, Saheb! Why would you spare any time or love for

someone like me? I'm the one who's crazy about you! You don't care at all!

Having said this, he laughed and pressed my hand as he shook it.

After this we met twice or thrice a week. On such occasions, he spoke excitedly about the progress of his new venture. Finally he filled his mini khakhras in a metal container and exported them. He then wrote letters asking about further requirements. Made phone calls. Ordered another lot to be made. And one fine day, disappeared with Khandwawala Baba.

When I visited his factory a couple of times, only the watchman was there.

I went again after about a month and saw that the factory was quite empty. Maganbhai sat in a corner reading a book. I thought he was studying formulae from a new chemistry book. But the book that he put aside when he saw me was *Dharmamanthan.*

He welcomed me lovingly, held my hand, asked me to sit next to him and said, I sent everything quite properly from here. The khakhras reached New York safe and sound. I tried calling Devdatt again and again, but he was never home. I also sent three, four telegrams and letters. Finally I phoned his friend. He told me that Devdatt has gone underground. The police were looking for him ... Our consignment of khakhras was getting stale in the customs ... Finally Devdatt was arrested and deported to India. He had gone there on a fake passport and green card ... He's not even bothered to meet me after he returned. The entire business collapsed. I paid off the women and sent them home. These days I'm reading *Dharmamanthan* and from time to time I go to Khandwawala Baba for enlightenment. Tell me, do you want to love me?

I nodded Yes. He picked up his copy of *Dharmamanthan* and locked up the factory.

We sat on my scooter and drove off to my house.

"Maganbhaino Gundar" was first published in *Etad*, 1999, and later as part of *Maganbhaino Gundar Ane Anya Vartao*, Vikalp Prakashan, Mumbai, 2001.

PAGES FROM A DIARY

24.9.1972

Should you happen to stop by the Ambika Mill and wish to see the boss, seek out Sundarlal first. His desk is right next to the air-conditioned cabin. Don't miss him. I specially recommend you to see him. He is a person worth meeting. You will not like his face from a distance. Ink-black complexion, inch deep hollows in both cheeks, yellow teeth, and they fall out as he laughs. Did I say Sundarlal is good looking? I said he was someone worth meeting. Sundarlal works hard in the office, and he has earned the Seth's confidence. When others leave the office at five thirty, Sundarlal continues to sit with the

Provident Fund ledgers. You would like to see the boss. The boss won't ask you to his cabin instantly. Have to wait outside for a while. There's a chair to sit on, no sofa. No old magazines to flick through to pass the time. Feel hesitant about striking up a conversation with a stranger, don't you? Sundarlal has been eyeing you for quite some time. Let your face be a little less stiff, if you look at him, he will tell you about the boss's moods – whether you should see him or not. If you get bored he will entertain you with gossip about the boss. That's why I say Do meet Sundarlal when you go to Ambika Mill. To our eyes he is not beautiful. His white cap off, specs down his nose, bending over the ledgers as he works, one gets a full view of his bushy hair. Once Arundhatiben told the boss in no uncertain words, I feel more attracted to Sundarlal's bushy hair than your porcupine hair.

Sundarlal spent the next seven days in a trance.

1.4.1985

It happened about the twentieth of March.

Nights, returning from work, I carry folks up to the station on my scooter. The station is on my way home from the downtown area. At times folks get sentimental, give their addresses, give thanks. At times, they get off and rush to the station without uttering a syllable.

I offered a lift to a man in a striped ash-coloured shirt and trousers standing near Jubilee Garden. He wanted to have a chat, so asked me to stop the scooter in Sayajigunj.

We sat on the steps of a house nearby. Ordered two cups of tea.

People call me Kumar saheb.

Are you headed for Bombay?

Yah.

Your bag?

Well, I *do* have Vijay Kumar's house!

Where do you stay?

If you wish to see me in Baroda I will be at the Vijay Adarsh Lodge, every evening at six. Tonight I leave for Bombay. Have organized an important programme. Rajiv will be there. Vijay Kumar and Rajiv Gandhi ... schoolmates in Delhi. He's given the responsibility to me. I will see Lataji and Ashaji. In fact I've just rung Laxmikant and R D.

When do you return?

In two days. For the time being give me five hundred rupees if you have it. I will return it to you when I come back.

I have just fifty.

Will do. See you.

Three days later I went to Vijay Adarsh Lodge at six.

Come, come ... So saying he bid me sit on the rope khatla.

You came back?

What can I say?

Why?

I have to go to Bombay today.

Again?

Yes, the programme is fixed to take place in Lalbag. Since Rajiv is to be there, the stage is big enough to take twenty five thousand. Vijay Kumar telephoned and decided it all. If Rajiv comes, all the film stars will definitely come. But Rajiv says that a portion will have to go for charity. I will make a hundred thousand or so.

Well, shall I push off then?

Want to go? What's the hurry? Let's go downstairs, have something to eat, and go sit in Jubilee Garden. My train does not leave until eleven.

We had tea – he ate. As soon as he finished eating, he made a quick exit. I paid the bill.

It was about seven when we sat down on a bench in Jubilee Garden.

Taking my hand in his, he said, You won't believe this ... and pressing my fingers asked, Guess how old I am?

Fifty five?

He roared with laughter. Got fooled, eh? Am a solid sixty five. I have abstained from sex for the last twenty years. Three or four times my wife became very passionate. I said, bathe waist down in cold water. I am a Shiva bhakta. This mark between my eyes is Shiva's third eye. It was this eye with which Kamadeva was burnt to ashes. I worship Shiva every night at eleven. Twice he was pleased with me and gave me darshana of his lotus feet.

He dropped my hand and entered the past. In Bombay a Parsi woman was crazy about me. She asked me to conjugate. I explained the story of Bhishma Pitamaha to her, and flatly said no to sex. You see? Meet me after three days. Of course, you have to give me the money for my fare to Bombay.

After a gap of three or four days I went to the lodge. With him there sat a fat young man in a black checked bush shirt, wearing thick glasses.

Kumar sahcb said, This is J P Patel. Owner of Shital Fans. Wants to go to Delhi. If he gets the licence his sales will be fifteen crores a year. Wants to make me his sleeping partner. The previous partner siphoned off twelve lakhs. Cheated J P. Now the factory is closed. We have go to Delhi.

When do you go?

We leave today. I told J P that as soon as Khakhar saheb comes we will get fifteen thousand. Vijay Kumar will reach there directly from Bombay. We will meet Rajiv and have Shital factory declared a sick unit. Rajiv is a friend of Vijay Kumar. He knows me too by name.

How come he knows you?

I had told Indiraji, You won't see 1985. That letter must

have gone to Rajiv. Vijay Kumar has been insisting on introducing me to Rajiv. But I told him, Forget it, such things are affairs of the mighty. I'm a small man.

I do not have fifteen thousand. Not now, not in my bank account either.

Get the money from your friends. Once the factory starts working there will be no problem at all.

Sorry, I don't think I can manage that.

If you give fifteen thousand today all problems can be solved. I had money in Bombay, but out of that I paid twenty five to Lata, twenty five to Laxmikant and fifteen to Asha. If I had not paid them J P's job would be through by now. As soon as he gets the licence, there's the machinery waiting in Germany all ready to be despatched. It will be useful for me too to get into a partnership without investing anything.

I stood up in order to get out of the question of giving him fifteen thousand. So, Kumar saheb quickly said, Come, I will go downstairs with you.

Then he turned to J P, Don't worry. I am there! I will fix your fifteen thousand.

Tea, like the last time, his quick exit and the bill paid, we settled down on a bench in Jubilee Garden. Again, taking my hand in his, he said, This whole month is the month of Shivashankar Bholenath. You know, it was forty years ago that I got married. In those days my intercourse with wife would last for half an hour. Others jump off in five minutes. From my very childhood I have been a Shiva devotee. In the Shravan month I wouldn't even look at a female. If you don't trust me, ask your bhabhi. She will tell you that I haven't touched her in the last twenty years. Well, once or twice I had a tremendous desire. Almost lost my head. Had thoughts of nothing but sex. Then I took cold water baths. Kept pouring water over my head for half hours, kept thinking of Shiva. Twice I have had the vision of Shiva's lotus feet. Shiva asked me to ask for a boon. I said, Release me from this cycle of births. Shiva said, You will get to live your next life in this very life. Khakhar saheb, do you see this bald head? Just wait till December. There will be dark hair. The body of a twenty five year old. You won't be able to recognize me. J P will keep waiting there and will cry. Now, no going back to the lodge tonight. Vijay Kumar will reach Delhi on the third. The meeting with Rajiv is on the fifth. Bye, Bye! See me in December. Well, now in my old age I must be of use to other people. Once Lataji's programme is over, I mean to take everybody with me to London, Paris, Moscow, New York. Khakhar saheb, I will buy your ticket too ... See you.

7.3.1987

When we left the Garden he was impatient to reach home. I was crossing the road slowly. Jitubhai had already crossed over, weaving his way between the rickshaws with not a worry for himself, then he waited on the other side impatiently. I was halfway to the other side and had just managed to avoid the last cyclist in my way, when he asked, Where is the scooter?

I said, Next to Acharya Book Depot. So we will have to go round the circle.

Come, walk a little faster.

He was soon standing near Acharya Book Depot. Immediately he said, Which scooter?

The grey one.

There are three here.

Here, this one.

I had to obey the authority in his commanding voice. I ripped out the scooter key from the back pocket of my trousers and started the scooter.

Which way?

The lane next to the fire brigade station.

Impatience, curiosity and the eagerness to arrive were Jitubhai's. That's why he had been commanding me. I too was aware that this relationship was to last no more than half an hour. Both of us would forget each other within a day. There was no joy nor excitement in my mind. There was a weariness, a monotony in the chain of happenings in such relationships.

I knew what kind of a house it would be. A house with a

rexine-covered sofa, a mini swing, a ceiling fan, and the walls painted white or grey ... Lost in thought, I reached the third floor. He had already climbed a staircase ahead of me. I saw him press the bell of room number 305. I climbed the stairs and stood behind Jitubhai. He too was breathless. The door opened three inches.

Jitubhai, Keys.

The door shut. Two minutes later a bunch of keys was held out by the fingers of a child. She wore bangles on her wrist. Jitubhai took the key.

He unlocked the house right opposite. Inside, an office table, under it a mattress gathered into a roll. Jitubhai switched on the fan. The glass window was shut. The typewriter on the table was covered. Since I wasn't certain where to sit, I pulled out the chair that was pushed into the space under the table and sat on it. The lower fringe of his shirt touched my mouth. Once in a while it flapped across my face when the wind blew.

Jitubhai, Wouldn't you like to stay here?

I shuddered at the thought of spending the night in that room with no ventilation. I lied, I have to catch the morning bus to Ahmedabad at six.

Go from here.

I have to collect some office papers from home. Besides, I haven't told my people at home, either.

We both knew that this first encounter was also the last

one. Jitubhai took off his cap and shirt and stood close to the chair. For the first time I looked at his face in the stark tubelight. An illness years ago had scarred it. The shining head, the sweat-drenched and pockmarked face looked ugly. Moreover, the thin lips made it look cruel too.

A hoarse voice emanated from the tall strong body.

The building gate closes at nine every night, so be quick.

With this he moved the typewriter with a jerk, and sat on the table. Before my eyes now the white vest, the white dhoti and the phallus that sprang from it. I looked up. The pockmarked cheeks had been smiling. Both eyes were shut to a slit, like the eyes of a Chinese.

He said, All well?

I said, Let's skip this today.

Jitubhai asked, Why?

Some other time.

You know as well as I do that ...

What?

We shall never meet again.

He caught my hand. Involvements, allurement, attraction had disappeared from my heart. I was thinking of paintings. A complete canvas full of the white vest, the white dhoti and the slight transparency that revealed the phallus. I tried to get up from the chair. He took my hand, made me sit and said,

What's wrong today?

I'm not in the mood.

What happened to your mood. Did I do something?

No, just feeling off.

Come on, for my sake.

I stayed there till nine for the sake of a man I would never meet again in my life.

"Dayarina Pana" was first published in *Gadyaparva* No 12, 1990, Baroda. This translation has been reproduced from *Katha Prize Stories*, Volume 2.

VADKI

Jamna lay flat on the bed, staring vacantly at the ceiling.

She was unhappy. She had diligently finished her chores – she did the sweeping, the laundering and the washing of utensils herself – since Jamnadas and she were the only members of the household.

Jamna and Jamnadas had entered into an agreement on their wedding night. The contractual document was on stamp paper, duly signed by both parties. Its contents covered every possible eventuality of their married life. Each of them preserved a copy of this document in a safe place.

So when late at night, in the throes of arousal, Jamna begged for a child, it was a copy of this document that Jamnadas brought out and read aloud from.

> **Section 9, Sub Section (a)**
> With this, the signatories of the contract, Jamnadas Bapalal and Jamna Jamnadas agree to abide by the decision that: Should any aspect of our personal relationship, be it embraces, kisses, foreplay, play, afterplay or joint read-aloud sessions of the erotic classics, result in the desire for a child, we shall consciously suppress all such activity/activities, bathe ceremoniously in cold water, uproot this desire, and banish it.

The reading and implementation of this Sub Section invariably proved to be an effective deterrent for desire of all kinds – including that for a child – and brought Jamna's feet down to earth, even metaphorically.

After much pondering and planning, Wednesdays and Saturdays were finalized for lovemaking. Jamna had expressed a desire to celebrate three days of intimacy in the place of just two before signing on the dotted line. The dialogue,

JAMNA. If you don't mind, could we amend Section 10, Sub Section (b)?

JAMNADAS. What amendment do you want to propose?

JAMNA. You have indicated Wednesday and Saturday for pleasures of the flesh. I feel that this programme should be scheduled thrice a week, say, every Thursday, Saturday and Sunday. That way the body would have more opportunities per week to partake in the play of Goddess Rati. I vote for Thursdays, Saturdays and Sundays.

JAMNADAS. Taking our youth into account, I am tempted to accept the proposed amendment. But consider this. My father Bapalal had to summon a carpenter the day he turned fifty. He had a double bed sawn into two right in front of our entire family.

JAMNA. Why?

JAMNADAS. Because the attraction he had once felt for Ba's body had waned. Energies had dwindled. From that day on, Bapuji's cot lay next to the window in the drawing room and Ba's bed was made in the inner room.

JAMNA. So what do you propose?

JAMNADAS. If it is wished that the capacity for pleasure should last, the principle of two days a week must be observed. And I would still say Wednesdays and Saturdays.

JAMNA. Why those days specifically?

JAMNADAS. Sunday being a holiday, we can sleep late on account of activities of mutual recreation. Mondays and Tuesdays come too soon after that.

JAMNA. Why not Thursdays?

JAMNADAS. Thursdays are for fasting. Weakened bodies generate Kama with difficulty.

So Section 10 (a) was constituted thus –

> **Section 10, Sub Section (a)**
> We, the husband-and-wife signatories of this document, hereby do declare that we will celebrate physical intimacies every Wednesday and Saturday till the time Jamnadas Bapalal turns fifty. If and when such an event comes to pass, Jamnadas has the option of calling a carpenter to saw the double bed into two.

The tragic look on Jamna's face at this time had inspired Jamnadas to compose a new clause –

> **Section 10, Sub Section (b)**
> In addition to the provisions made in Section 10 (a), we, the signatories of this document, agree to consider the option of celebrating Full Moon, No Moon, Moon-in-the-Sixth-Phase (ascendant and descendant), and Birthday Nights by mutual consent.

After the inclusion of this Sub Section, Jamna had happily agreed to Wednesdays and Saturdays.

Today their marital life is a happy one because they have strictly adhered to the Sections and Sub Sections of this document. Jamnadas is fifty two and yet no carpenter has as much as touched their double bed. Because of his foresight they still continue to celebrate Wednesdays and Saturdays, not to mention the odd night covered under Section 10, Sub Section (b).

But something has just marred the golden platter of their bliss. Where *is* her vadki?

Normally Jamna's heart fluttered every Saturday. But this afternoon she lay on the bed staring sadly at the ceiling. Her mind was churning like an inferno. When Jamnadas had come home for lunch, she had hardly noticed that he had winked – an acknowledgment of it being a Saturday. He had spoken of irrelevant issues like the soaring rates at the stock exchange, as he slurped noisily through his kadhi. After lunch he had extracted a Cavender's from his pocket and blown clouds of smoke all over the room. But no smile had appeared on Jamna's lips. Usually Jamna liked to see Jamnadas smoking. She'd say, When you wear goggles and smoke cigarettes, you look just like Ashok Kumar.

But Jamna's mind was elsewhere as she lay on the bed. She was thinking that her neighbours were solely responsible for her sorrow, and yet, how many households did she have associations with? One could easily count these on one's fingertips. There were thirty families in Badrikashram and she had dealings with only six of them.

Among the six too, it was only with Savita she had a relationship just-like-home. But she too had not been around the last two days. She had said that she was going home to her bhai-and-bhabhi's house. God only knew where she had really gone. Savita had an old and vicious enmity with her bhabhi and just two years ago she had taken a vow to never go there. So where had she gone? With whom had she gone? Whose eyes did she think she was throwing mud in? Along with the missing vadki, these questions also perturbed Jamna.

It was two o'clock on Saturday afternoon. Savita had returned home just this morning so she was still busy with the household chores. When Vimla came to meet her, she was cleaning the kitchen floor with a wet rag. Seeing Vimla at her doorstep Savita was worried, the cross-examination would soon begin.

SAVITA. *Worthless woman, who are you to stand there asking questions? What have I to do with you?* Welcome Vimlaben, I was just thinking of coming over to your place after I finished the cleaning.

VIMLA. I just finished my chores. Your bhai has left for office and since I hadn't seen your face for many days, I thought I'd come over.

SAVITA. *What's there to see in my face? Don't I know that you have come to cross-examine me?* I too was keen to meet you.

VIMLA. *Liar! You'd never want to meet me! Where were you for two days? I want to know that!* How are Bhai-Bhabhi?

SAVITA. *Just two days out of town and you get a stomach ache, don't you?* If there's illness at home is it not one's duty to go? Bhabhi was unwell, so I went.

VIMLA. *Rascal, you've been absconding for two days! Who have you seduced this time?* It's a woman's lot. One has to clean utensils, whether it is at one's husband's place or at one's brother's place. But how's Bhabhi now?

SAVITA. If there's no letter in fifteen days, I'll have to go again.

VIMLA. *So! She's fixed everything!* I used to ask my brother's wellbeing everyday.

SAVITA. *Don't I know that? You just love acting coy while talking to other women's husbands.* He never tires of praising you. You took great care of him. (*Changing the topic ...*) Jamna had come over.

VIMLA. *You changed the topic, didn't you? You cunning bitch!* Yes. Her vadki is lost.

SAVITA. What does she think? Am I a vadki-thief? Just three days back I'd returned her vadki – why does she come swinging her big bum to ask questions every now and again? Are all of us thieves and is she the only honest person?

VIMLA. You know her nature.

SAVITA. I don't have to take this from her in this birth!

VIMLA. She is suspicious of everyone. If anyone so much as talks to Jamnadas she comes and stands between them like a shield.

SAVITA. *Don't I know your doings?* Twice already she's snooped around my kitchen, and yet this morning at eight she again dropped in to coo like a koel!

VIMLA. Your just-like-home relationship has lasted with Jamna because of your good nature.

SAVITA. Everyone in the chawl avoids her like she has rabies.

VIMLA. Jamna was petty-minded right from the beginning. Just because she loses one wretched vadki, she's taken on the entire Badrikashram.

SAVITA. *When you'd lost your sandsi, you'd left no stone unturned to pick quarrels with "the entire Badrikashram." Daily searches, surprise-checkings and cross-examinations!* You too had inquired once or twice when you'd lost your sandsi.

VIMLA. If it is fated that one is to have a utensil one can never lose it.

SAVITA. *How could you have lost it? Everyone knew that you were taking hot almond-milk for that Shivlal.* Where did you find the sandsi eventually?

VIMLA. *Don't tell me you don't remember!* You were the one who tattled all over the chawl that I used to take milk and jalebies for Shivlal.

SAVITA. It was such a long time ago that I forgot.

VIMLA. *Surely she has seduced someone. The question is who? I must find out!* God! If little Jaglo asks for a snack this afternoon I have nothing prepared and here I am, sitting and chitchatting with you.

Jamna got up from the bed. She opened the drawer of her desk and took out a pencil and paper. She sharpened the pencil with a pen-knife, sat on the chair and wrote thus,

20/3. Monday. When I had taken batata pauva in the vadki to Savita's place in the afternoon, she was sitting on the swing stitching buttons to a pair of pyjamas.

22/3. Wednesday. At nine o'clock in the morning, when I had started to steam the dal to make vedhmis, Bankumasi came over and borrowed a vadkiful of flour. She must have been in a hurry. She did not even stay for a chat. She'd sent Tapu to return the vadki in the evening.

23/3. Thursday. Jaglo had come from Vimlaben's place to borrow the silver vadki and achmani. They had held Satyanarayan pooja in the evening. The vadki and achmani were returned at nine o'clock that night. The achmani was sparkling clean and the vadki was full of sheera.

25/3. Saturday. Vimlaben had come in the evening to borrow melvan. I gave her a spoonful. She returned the spoon the next morning.

26/3. Sunday. Savita had sent a vadkiful of dal. According to her, that vadki was mine. Bankumasi was here when the vadki arrived. She remembers a vadki, but she does not remember what it looked like. I never use vadkis with upturned edges.

29/3. Wednesday. Savita doesn't even need a reason to pick a quarrel. When I had asked her about the vadki, she had snorted. With an air of injured innocence she had asked, Do we want to make our money by stealing your vadki? Just two years ago, she had borrowed my cloth bag to buy vegetables. What had happened then? When I had asked for the bag three, four times, hadn't she pretended as if she knew nothing about cloth bags? Wasn't it a nightmare to recover the bag from her? The liar just loves to shove everything under her big bottom.

1/4. Saturday. Just decided. There's only one solution. I'll give five peppermints to Vimlaben's Jaglo and send him to all the five houses to check their vadkis. If it is still not found, I will personally inspect their kitchens.

She tied the piece of paper at one end of her sari and lay down on the bed again. Suddenly there was a knock on the door. Think of the devil and ... It was Satan! In person. Smartly dressed. With hair styled to resemble an upturned straw broom, carrying a top in one hand and a piece of string in the other.

JAMNA. I was just thinking of you.

JAGLO (*unstrings the spinning top in his palm with a flourish*). Ah, then you must have a job for me.

JAMNA. Jagla, do you want a peppermint?

JAGLO. You only offer peppermints when you want to get something done. (*Draws an imaginary sword from an imaginary scabbard at his waist.*) We are not entertained. We reject your plea. (*Abandons the imaginary hardware.*) What's the job? The going rate for delivering Savitakaki's letters is one rupee a letter. The days are over when peppermints could get any real work done.

JAMNA. Twenty five paise.

JAGLO. We are not beggars. Don't even bother to mention less than eight anna in our presence.

JAMNA. To whom did you take Savita's letters?

JAGLO. One rupee for telling the name. Fixed rate. Now, what was it that you wanted?

JAMNA (*rises and opens the cupboard*). I'll give you the rupee but you'll have to tell me everything. You'll get the eight annas after you do my job.

JAGLO (*pockets the rupee*). Last week I'd gone to Vithal Sadan across the street to hand over her letter to Shantilal. We have our ethics. I've not told anyone else about this. Now, what's your assignment?

JAMNA. See. I'll write down the names of five families in our chawl. All you have to do is to go to their kitchens and check the names inscribed on all their vadkis. Then come back and tell me if the name on any vadki is Jamnadas Bapalal.

JAGLO. This is a lot of work. The minimum charge for this assignment is one rupee. I'll have to take the kids from all these houses into confidence.

JAMNA. Okay. You'll get a rupee. But I need to know this by the 2nd. *So, Savita has started a correspondence with Shantilal! It wouldn't surprise me if he was the one she was with the last couple of days. The minute Shantilal's wife left for her mother's place to have her baby there, Savita has gone and infiltrated the household. One never knows about the human heart: who'll fall in love with whom and fall out of love too.*

Every Saturday night, Jamna burnt incense, lit perfumed agarbattis in three corners, wore a veni in her hair, cooked dal dhokli for supper and switched off the lights early. Saturday and Wednesday nights Jamnadas did not go to have his smoke in the veranda with the menfolk of Badrikashram.

Today, when Jamnadas sat for dinner, there was no dal dhokli. From the time they got married, the fixed menu for every Saturday night was dal dhokli and for every Wednesday night, vedhmi. Jamna would add extra leaven in the dhokli to make it soft as pooris. She would spread several teaspoons of ghee on the vedhmi and serve it enthusiastically, often cajoling him to eat more than he wanted to. Today there was no enthusiasm, no cajoling, no love. Jamnadas ate hastily, eyes downcast. He washed his hands and, while chopping betelnuts, he finally began the conversation.

JAMNADAS. What's the matter? Why do you look so upset? (*Without uttering a word Jamna went to the sink to put away the dishes.*)

JAMNADAS. I say, why are you angry with me? Have you forgotten today is Saturday?

JAMNA. Who says I am angry with you?

JAMNADAS. Then why was I punished with gourd-and-potato vegetable? Is it not the day for dal dhokli?

JAMNA. I know what day it is.

JAMNADAS. You know very well that I can't stand this sickly gourd-and-potato.

JAMNA. When I put away the dishes I noticed that you had not even touched it.

JAMNADAS. Then what's the matter with you?

JAMNA. Go ask your neighbours of Badrikashram. They have not spared me any sorrow.

JAMNADAS. What happened?

JAMNA. Ask me what has not happened!

JAMNADAS. Consider it asked.

JAMNA. You remember, we went to buy a set of stainless steel vadkis on dhanteras five years ago?

JAMNADAS. When was that?

JAMNA. When Nitu was born at Motabhai's house. That year

you had fractured your hand during Navratri. The same year, on dhanteras we had bought a set of six vadkis for eighty rupees.

JAMNADAS. So what about them?

JAMNA. Well, I can't find one vadki of that set.

JAMNADAS. Never mind, we will buy a new one.

JAMNA. Such sets are not available anymore.

JAMNADAS. We'll buy a better set. Don't worry yourself over it.

JAMNA. So if someone swallows our vadkis, we're supposed to just run out and buy a new set, is it? I want the same vadki and I want to find out who has stolen it.

JAMNADAS. You go on breaking your head over it. I will not interfere. Let me know when you want a new set.

Jamnadas made a paan and placed it in his cheek. He then sat for half an hour in the veranda. That night both of them slept with their backs facing each other. Jamna lay awake for some time thinking that a woman who could steal somebody's husband would not be ashamed to steal a vadki.

On the evening of the 2nd, Jaglo arrived with disastrous news. He reported that he had thoroughly investigated all the five families listed. None of the kitchens had a vadki with *Jamnalal Bapalal* inscribed on it. Jaglo asked for a hike in his fees. One and a half rupees. In four of the houses he had to use bribes of upto four peppermints to get the job done by his friends. This assignment had proved to be a total loss for him. Should Jamna not give him the one and a half rupees at once, then he would be compelled to write *Savita Vadkichor* on the walls of Badrikashram. Since everyone in the chawl knew that it was Jamna who had recently lost a vadki, she would be the prime suspect as the sponsor of such a campaign. This would only give Jamna a bad name.

But Jamna had the tact to convert any situation to her advantage. She played with one and a half rupees in her palm and said, I will give you the money. You have worked for it. But you will have to tell me where Savita and Shantilal meet.

Jaglo's eyes were riveted to the coins. While returning from the evening darshan they meet in the garden of Madhavbagh. Having said this, he put the coins in his pocket and left.

Jamna began to think. She remembered that when she had gone to give batata pauva to Savita, she was stitching buttons on a pair of pyjamas. Savita's husband always wore a dhoti and her kids always wore half-pants. Surely the pyjamas must be Shantilal's. Then she remembered the conversation she had had when she had met Savita that evening.

SAVITA. I am never able to cook such soft batata pauva.

JAMNA. *If you are a miser with oil what else do you expect?* There is nothing to it. Everyone cooks this way. Don't flatter me unnecessarily.

SAVITA. So I may be flattering you unnecessarily, but why would Shantilal lie in such a small matter?

JAMNA. Shantilal?

SAVITA. The one who lives in that grand flat in Vithal Sadan across the street.

If the vadki had reached Shantilal's house, Jamna felt she would never get it back. Jamna thought it over for the twenty second time. When Bankumasi had come over to borrow the flour, her eyes were moist. She had not even stayed back to chat for a couple of minutes. The poor, unhappy woman! Her husband beat her up regularly for no fault of hers. Yet she was so considerate! That very evening her son Tapu returned the flour in the same vadki. Even his face was lacklustre. He had not even stopped to taste the freshly cooked vedhmi filling.

On the evening of the 25th, Vimlaben had come to borrow some melvan. She had stayed back to gossip.

VIMLA. Your vadki must be at Savita's place.

JAMNA. I've been there twice. The house was locked.

VIMLA. She was saying that her bhai and bhabhi have called her over.

JAMNA. How can that be? She does not get along with her bhabhi at all.

VIMLA. Then where do you think she has gone?

JAMNA. You can never tell with her. She aims at one target and scores a bull's eye on another.

VIMLA. When my sandsi was lost, remember all that happened afterwards? I would have to lift hot pots of vegetable, milk and rice with a rag. Ten days later, it was found at Shivlalbhai's house.

JAMNA. *The whole town knows how crazy you are about Shivlal.* Is that so? Had you found it at Shivlalbhai's place? I had simply forgotten.

VIMLA. *You are no less than Savita.* It's been over two years. That is why you forgot. Remember, you'd sent the silver vadki and achmani to my place on the day of the Satyanarayan pooja?

JAMNA. I also remember that you had taken the trouble to return the vessels filled with prasad. Why, you had returned the melvan spoon ... In the last month I have not even sent the tiffin to anyone. See there it sits and yawns.

VIMLA. Savita is very careless by nature.

JAMNA. Her intentions are not good. It was a pain to get my cloth bag back from her. I had sent the vadki with the batata pauva. Now it has gone directly to Shantilal's house. We'll never get it back.

VIMLA. Shantilal?

JAMNA. I don't know him. Savita was saying, he has a grand flat across the street on the first floor of Vithal Sadan.

VIMLA. Yes, I have seen him. Savita is too much. She can bring down a flying bird. We would not even notice the bird.

JAMNA. I still don't know anything about Shantilal. But it is a fact that in front of your brother she likes to dress up and simper.

On Sunday the 2nd, Jamna sat watching *Ramayana* with a view to follow the adventures of the ideal woman. But Jamnadas observed that her eyes would often stray towards the door. Just as Ram assembled his army of monkeys on the opposite shores of Ravan's Lanka, Vimlaben dropped in. She signalled to Jamna who slithered out of the room so as to not disturb Jamnadas.

VIMLA. She had just come over to leave her key at my place.

JAMNA. Did she say anything?

VIMLA. No. Her Highness was in full regalia. Chiffon saree, lipstick and reeking of perfume. When she handed over the key to me, she looked like a fragrant honeycomb.

JAMNA. Where has she gone! When will she return?

VIMLA. She has gone over to Shantilal's to watch *Ramayana* on his colour television. So she will be back when it is over at 10:15 am.

JAMNA. Such dressing up just to go across the street?

VIMLA. She has gone to throw mud in Shantilal' eyes.

JAMNA. Then let us get it over with.

VIMLA. I will keep a watch near the parapet. If anyone comes your way I will cough three times.

JAMNA. And I will come out immediately.

VIMLA. Take care though that no one notices you.

Jamna opened the lock to Savita's house and entered. She started with the kitchen. Shelves, sinks, pots, pans, oil containers, the ghee vadki, the grain bin – inside, outside, everywhere. Around none of this could she find the vadki bearing Jamnadas's name. In the living room she examined the table, the chair, the lamp, the book, the file, the wrist watch, the carpet, the double bed and the table fan. Disappointment here too. She searched the store room, the bathroom, the latrine all over. Half-an-hour later when she emerged, Jamna looked like a sadhu, a layer of ash on her face.

VIMLA. Who are you?

JAMNA. It's me.

VIMLA. What is this you have done to your face?

JAMNA. The whole house is covered with dust. If she had any time left from wandering all over town only then would she find time to take care of her own house. The stray bitch!

VIMLA. Did you find it?

JAMNA. No.

VIMLA. She may have hidden it somewhere.

JAMNA. I went through every corner of her house with a tooth comb. My vadki is not in this house.

VIMLA. Come along. It is time we left, she will be here any moment like an angel of death.

Sunday evening was also the same – Jamna lay defeated on the bed staring vacantly at the white ceiling. Jamnadas could not bear to see her so unhappy. He sat on the bed and took Jamna's head in his lap.

JAMNADAS. Why do you torture yourself? If the vadki has gone we'll buy a new one. Why do you worry your precious self over this trivial matter and make me so unhappy?

JAMNA. Do I complain if they eat our soft-soft batata pauva? But I simply cannot bear anyone devouring the vadki with it. I don't want to live in Badrikashram any more. Find us rooms in another chawl.

JAMNADAS. There will be neighbours in every chawl, and you'll feel lonely in a flat.

Jamnadas got up from the bed and brought a glass of water for Jamna. She refused it with a shake of her head. He switched on the television because it was time for the Sunday feature film. It was an Ashok Kumar film. If any other day, Jamna had known of an Ashok Kumar film, she would have served dinner right in front of the television set. Nothing diverts her from her grief today, thought Jamnadas as he watched the film distractedly.

In the film a nautch girl dances and sings. Pretending to

be drunk, Ashok Kumar sidles up to her. The girl surreptitiously slips something in his palm and whispers in his ear. He staggers out. When he reaches the ground floor Ashok Kumar straightens up, abandons his pretense and knocks on a door. He passes the object to someone inside and walks away.

Watching this, Jamnadas started. He leaped up from his chair as if a scorpion had bitten him. He put on his chappals and ran down the staircase two steps at a time just like Jaglo. He reached the ground floor and knocked on Shivlal's door. The door opened. Shivlal's hair was dyed a deep black.

SHIVLAL. Welcome! Why did you leave the film halfway through?

JAMNADAS. Shivlal! I was given a choice. Either to see the film or to see Jamna's funeral!

SHIVLAL. Whatever happened?

JAMNADAS. She is on hunger strike.

SHIVLAL. Good for her. She needs to lose weight.

JAMNADAS. Here I am so troubled and you want to tease me!

SHIVLAL. Unless you tell me how will I know what is bothering you?

JAMNADAS. Do you remember – last week you needed some oil when you were making chappattis?

SHIVLAL. So?

JAMNADAS. I'd brought it with me when I'd come to sit in the veranda.

SHIVLAL. I remember. That night Jamna had gone to do the garba.

JAMNADAS. Well, that vadki is lost.

SHIVLAL. But it must be right here. Sit down, I'll find it.

Shivlal went to the kitchen and started knocking pots and pans around to search for the vadki.

JAMNADAS. Have you found it?

SHIVLAL. I am looking.

JAMNADAS. If you can't find it the world will end.

SHIVLAL. The vadki must surely be at Vimla's place. I will ask her to take it to your place tomorrow.

When Jamnadas returned, the television was on and Jamna was fast asleep.

On the afternoon of Monday, the 3rd, while sipping his buttermilk, Jamnadas asked with studied casualness,

JAMNADAS. So what happened to that vadki? Could you find it.

JAMNA. Vimlaben returned it this morning.

JAMNADAS. Now you must be relieved.

JAMNA. What relief?

JAMNADAS. Why, what happened?

JAMNA. It would have been better if I had not found the vadki.

JAMNADAS. What went wrong?

JAMNA. It was found at Shivlal's place.

JAMNADAS. How?

JAMNA. Who knows how it ended up there? I can't stand the sight of the man. The way he speaks, with emphasis on every word, that sophisticated whisper of his and that ghastly dye in his hair. I feel like slapping him.

JAMNADAS. The fellow seems okay to me.

JAMNA. You are really naive. Vimla would not hesitate to set fire to her own house over him. Get the message?

JAMNADAS. Why?

JAMNA. Vimla will now feel that I have a special relationship with Shivlal. If the vadki had not been found I would not be the target of such suspicion.

JAMNADAS. Have I accused you of anything?

JAMNA. I will have to get to the bottom of this. How did the vadki reach there?

JAMNADAS. Forget it. We found the vadki. It is enough.

JAMNA. Your wish is my command.

Jamnadas heaved a sigh of relief.

"Vadki" was first published in English in *The Bombay Literary Review*, Vol I, No 1, 1990. This translation has been reproduced from *Wordsmiths, A Katha Profile*.

PHOREN SOAP

This phoren soap is something else. Jeevanlal mumbled as he drew the hot water bucket closer and rubbed the soap on his head. He rubbed his hands, worked up a lather, caressed the foam around his thighs and crotch. He then poured a tumbler of hot water over his head. His hair stuck flat on his forehead. He rubbed the soap in his armpits, on his heels and between his toes. Cleansed the whole body. Of all its sins.

He called out to his wife, Savli, listen!

Savita shouted back, Why yell from the bathroom? Breakfast will be ready in five minutes.

Don't you ever think of anything except food? Jeevanlal

grumbled as he wrapped a red safi around his waist and emerged from the bathroom.

In a honeyed voice, he said, Savli darling, the perfume of this phoren soap is too much! As if it unlocks the gates of Heaven.

The batata pauva is ready. Savita answered as if she had not heard a word.

To hell with your batata pauva. We spend a lifetime eating sev usal and pau bhaji and whatnot. Where does that get us in life? Now here comes this phoren soap. Just look at it. This changes our whole damned life!

So, you don't want to eat?

To hell with your breakfast! Didn't I say I don't want it? Having made his point, Jeevanlal attacked the plate of batata pauva with gusto. He polished off the plateful in one go and took a swig of water.

Don't you dare tell anyone about the phoren soap! He got dressed and left for his office.

Jeevanlal had hardly descended the staircase when Savita started toying with the soap. How dare Jeevanlal forbid her! He has got into the habit of staking his claim on each and every thing in the house! As if he goes and fetches piles and piles of money for household expenses! Now she has to show this soap to somebody!

She smiled to herself as an idea flashed across her mind.

She wrapped the wet soap in its cover, tucked it inside her blouse, locked the house and went to Sharada's house.

Sharada was busy washing the dishes when Savita crossed her threshold and announced, You can't imagine what I've brought today. Just try to guess.

Sharada gaped at her.

Savita continued. It's not a pendant. Not a sari, nor a dining table.

A cordless telephone! Sharada gave voice to her own desire.

Savita shook her head, slipped a hand inside her blouse and fished out the bar resting in her cleavage. Polishing it with a corner of her sari, she placed the soap in the centre of the table and said, This is it. Soap. The real thing. My husband's nephew brought it from Abu Dhabi.

Sharada's eyes were riveted on the smiling blonde beauty posing with a cake of soap in her hand. The blonde's windswept hair seemed to shimmer. Transfixed, Sharada picked up the bar, inhaled its fragrance deeply and mumbled breathlessly, Savita, my friend, let me keep this soap for just one night. I'll return it in the morning when the milkman comes.

But don't you dare use it! Savita was wary.

You're always suspicious. I'll look after your soap as if it was an heirloom!

Promise?

Promise.

Savita's gaze drifted to the photograph of Sharada and Manilal hanging on the wall near the table. Smiling to herself she returned home.

Sharada woke up from her siesta at three. She looked under her pillow for the comely blonde on the soap wrapper. She put her nose close to the eyes of the fair, haughty woman and inhaled. She closed her eyes with a sigh.

She was up again in minutes. Going into the kitchen she placed three bucketfuls of water on the stove. No one else was at home. Sharada undressed before the mirror. Swaying her breasts, she spoke in the husky voice of a film star, Maniya, darling, see how beautiful and smooth my breasts are. I've been waiting for years for you to fondle them, to smell the perfume of my hair. And you? How do you make love? As if you are catching a train at the last minute!

She massaged her breasts, pushed them up and preened.

Flinging a towel over her shoulders she went into the bathroom. While bathing, her daily chant was unusually punctuated, *A dip in the Ganges, a dip in the Gomti, a dip in the Yamuna.* Where are you hiding, you goon? You are just insatiable. *A dip in the Tapti, a dip in the Triveni ...* Why are you hiding? Whom do you entice with your golden locks, you slut? *A dip in the Narmada, a dip in the Saraswati, a dip in the Godavari.* You are a slippery customer, you want to sneak deep inside.

Intoxicated by the fragrance, Sharada kept moaning to herself. As she rubbed the bar all over her body, she pressed it and pushed it into intimate places. She caught it between her legs and then flung it up in a way that it landed upon her breasts. She nestled it between her breasts and started pouring tumblers of water over her body. She finished all three bucketfuls of water and stepped out.

She picked up the wrapper from the table, wrapped it carefully around the bar, wiped it dry with her towel and put it away in her jewellery box. She returned to the bathroom to put on her sari.

Just then, Manilal returned from the office. He hung his khadi topi on the peg, sat on the bed and bellowed, Sharada! O Sharadee! What is this new smell? Why doesn't the house smell of garlic today?

Shaking her wet tresses, Sharada moved closer to Manilal. From her fragrant trance, she could discern that Manilal had pulled her to him with an excited gesture.

Unable to contain his urgency at five in the evening, Manilal asked, Tell me, please, what's all this?

You know ... Jeevanlal has brought a magic soap. Even its touch is mesmerizing. When you bathe with it, you acquire an uncontrollable attraction for the opposite sex. Go for a bath right away. I'll heat some water for you, She opened her jewellery box and said, Time is Money!

As soon as he saw the wrapper, Manilal exclaimed, What a woman!

Sharada said, Just look at it. Isn't it smooth and big!

When Manilal turned to the bathroom playing with the soap, Sharada said, Just have some patience. Let me get some hot water for you!

Manilal rubbed the soap over his penis as he bathed. His penis yawned, stretched and perked up as if it was struggling to recall the long forgotten state of erection. Manilal shut his eyes to conjure up a fantasy about Savita.

One evening Manilal returns home from office. The house is locked. He goes to Savita's house. Savita is mending Jeevanlal's kurta. She looks up, sees Manilal and speaks with the thread between her teeth, Sharada's gone to her mother's place. She'll be home late tonight. She's kept your dinner ready.

Manilal asks casually, Where's Jeevanlal?

He's busy with the audit in his office. He won't be back before eight.

Manilal makes his move, When I saw you stitching, I remembered – I too have a button missing on a kurta.

Savita takes the thread out of her mouth and says, You go home. I'll come over when I finish this.

Manilal leaves with his key.

Bare chested, wearing only a dhoti, Manilal sits watching

2/50

television as Savita enters with a needle and thread. She asks, Where's your kurta?

Manilal gets up from the chair. Savita stares at his hairy chest.

Manilal shifts his gaze from the television to Savita's breasts. Savita asks again, Where is the kurta and where is the missing button?

Manilal gets up and closes the main door. On the television, Mansukh Mali explains the methods of spreading compost in the garden. Manilal is about to turn the television off, but Savita stops him with a gesture saying, Let it be on. I like noise.

Savita sits on his bed. Manilal drops his kurta into Savita's lap.

Savita asks pointedly, Which button is missing?

For years it's been missing, but no one has the time to fix it.

Don't say such things. I too am attracted to your hairy chest. About three years ago when I dropped in here, you were in your vest, having a meal. I saw your chest for the first time then. I haven't forgotten the sight. But after all, Sharada is my best friend. I can't betray her.

Meanwhile, on the television, Mansukh explains how to add potash to manure. Manilal shuts him up with the mute button of the remote and says, She may be your best friend. But she's my only wife. And what can I do if her body is stuffed with ice cubes. She has never satisfied me.

Manilal pulls Savita closer. She hides herself in the night of his hairy chest and whispers, Doesn't Sharada know how to fix a button?

She doesn't know how to break a heart, either. With this, he plants a passionate kiss on her cheek.

Not so hard. I'll get a zit.

Savita lies flat on the bed. The room is filled with the moonlight glow of the television. Manilal keeps gazing at Savita. How rosy are her cheeks, he thinks, I want to bite them!

What are you waiting for? Savita is impatient.

I better take off my underpants, no?

Jeevanlal stopped using underpants three years ago.

Eyes shut tight, Manilal conjured up the entire sequence. He went over the whole fantasy, delighting in every detail.

As Manilal was climbing the ladder of ecstasy – penis in hand, enveloped in the warmth of the steam and the aroma of the soap – there was a knocking on the door.

Shaken out of his trance, Manilal yelled, What is it? Who's there?

Papa, it's me, a voice came through.

Who's me? Manilal was incapable of recognizing his son's voice in this state.

Your only son, Deepak!

Deepak who?

Your son.

Manilal's penis slackened a little in his hand.

What kind of a house is this? Can't I have a bit of peace even when I have a bath!

Deepak persisted, But Papa, I'm in a hurry.

What did you say?

I'm in a hurry. I have to go! Please open the dooooor.

Leave me alone for a few minutes. At least once in a while.

What can I do? I've got to gooooo.

Stop eating bhel puri. What filthy habits you have. Never wake up before ten in the morning.

But I studied till two past midnight for my exams! Oh, Oh!

Sharada, who had spent two hours and three bucketfuls of water over her bath, butted in, What can the poor boy do, hahn?

Didn't I tell him to stop eating ragda patties and drink a spoonful of castor oil once a week? Manilal took a last-ditch stand.

Sharada didn't take it lying down, How does it matter now, hahn?

His tummy will behave itself. Is this evening hour the time to go to the toilet?

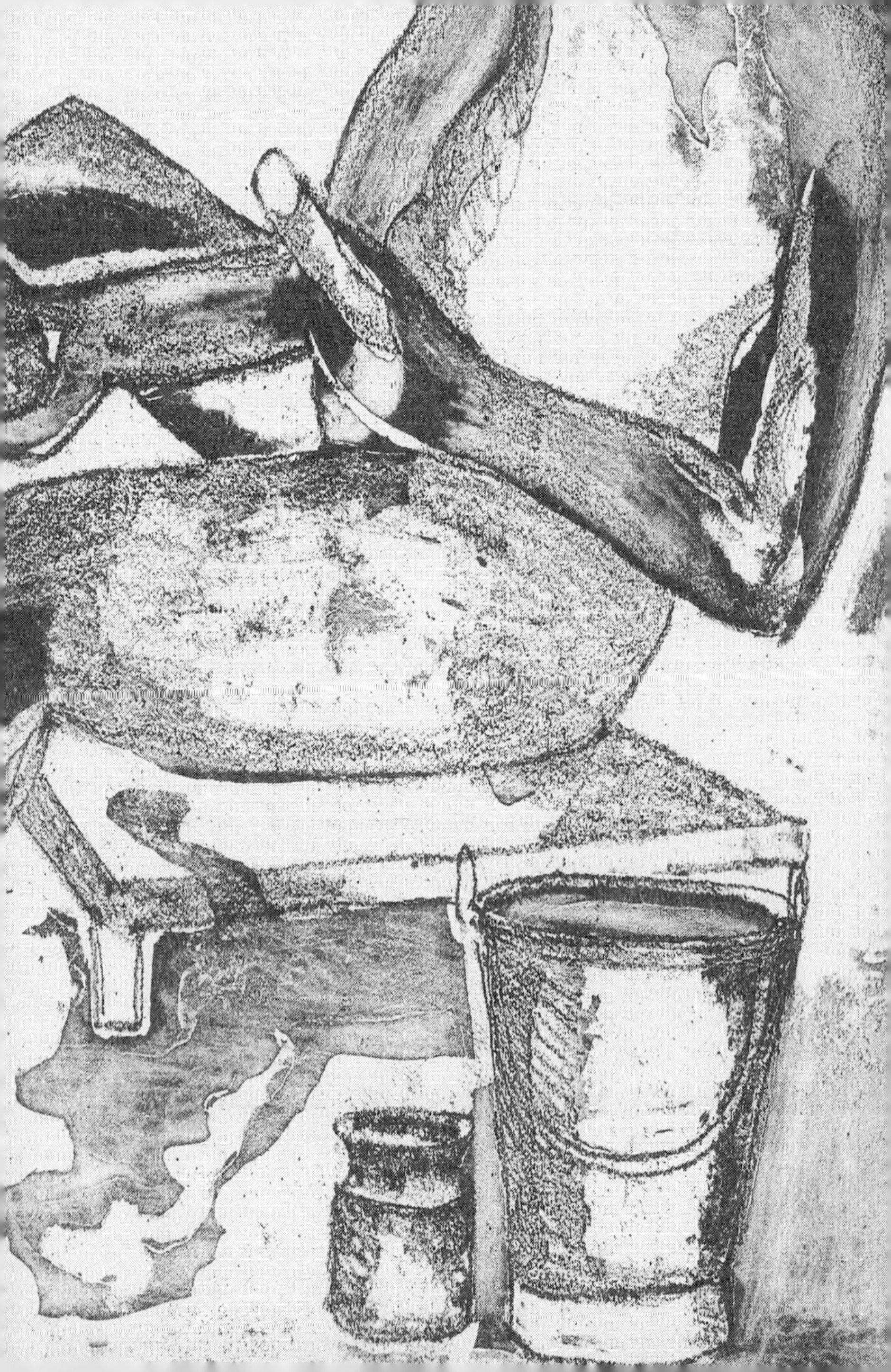

What are we before the forces of nature, hahn?

Pleeeeeease, Papa. Be quick, yelled Deepak as he rattled the bathroom door.

The key to ecstasy slipped out of Manilal's hand. Mumbling to himself, he wrapped a towel around his waist and undid the latch.

Deepak was hopping restlessly. As soon as the door opened, he rushed into the bathroom. Manilal was coming out. The two collided. Deepak slipped on the smooth, white bathroom tiles. As he fell, he tried to grab Manilal. But instead of Manilal, he caught hold of his towel. Deepak fell on the tiles pulling off Manilal's towel with him.

As he looked up from the floor, Deepak felt ashamed to look at his father's dark, ungainly body and his bulging belly. Manilal was stunned to be so exposed before his own son. He did not even have the presence of mind to pick up the towel.

Sharada was drying her hair in the living room, when she saw Manilal naked. She was bewildered at first. Then she burst out laughing. Unable to control her laughter, she collapsed in a chair, tittering. Manilal entered the room to pick up the dhoti hanging from a peg to cover his nakedness. Seeing the dark and yellow nudity of Manilal in the evening light, Sharada was reminded of a calendar picture of Ramdas Swami.

Deepak closed the bathroom door. He squatted contemplatively on the footrests of the white toilet, comparing

Manilal's dark semi-erect penis with his own fair little one. When he looked up, his eyes fell on the soap and the leftover bucket of hot water. After he had finished, he decided to have a bath.

When Deepak emerged from the bathroom with Manilal's towel wrapped around his waist, the cake of soap was reduced to the size of an eight anna coin. He went to the balcony and whistled.

Tommy came up wagging his tail. When Manilal saw Tommy, he could suppress his anger no more, What's this no good filthy creature doing here?

Tommy started barking the moment he saw Manilal.

Just then Sharada brought a glass of cold rose sherbet for Manilal. Manilal picked out an ice cube from the glass and hurled it at Tommy. Tommy ran into the bathroom, tail between his legs.

Deepak shut the door and rubbed the remaining soap on Tommy.

Soon enough, the eight anna sized soap fulfilled its karma and vanished from this world.

That night Jeevanlal had a strange dream. Soapsuds floated in the air, like the dance sequence of a Hindi film. He could see a variety of birds and beasts in the sea of foam and soapsuds. Ganapati, who sat at the centre, flung a bar of soap at a humanoid bird. The bird caught it in its beak and flew to the serpent Shesha on whose hood rested the globe. He saw Manilal in the place of Vishnu, lying on the bed of coiled serpents. Savita was shampooing Manilal's legs with the soap. Jeevanlal woke up with a start, flabbergasted.

Next morning, at six o'clock, the milkman delivered three bottles of milk at Savita's door. She left the door ajar for Sharada to return the soap discreetly. But soon it was seven. And no sign of Sharada. God, what will I say when Jeevanlal asks for it, thought Savita. I've no one but myself to blame for this catastrophe.

Finally, at a quarter past seven, she placed a green bar of Hamam in the bathroom and lighted the gas to heat the bath water.

Jeevanlal, as he brushed his teeth, roared from the bathroom, Savita, listen! Where's my soap? Where is my pink phoren soap? He flung the green Hamam out.

Savita, realizing she had lost, said, Forgive me, please.

For what? Jeevanlal asked furiously.

You warned me. But I couldn't resist the temptation of showing it to Sharada.

Why?

Sharada had never seen a phoren soap before.

So what happened?

She asked if she could borrow it from me.

What for?

She wanted to keep it under her pillow while she slept.

When did she say she would return it?

She promised to return it this morning, before the milkman arrived.

It's already morning. We've had two cups of tea! So where is the soap?

I wonder.

Go, get it right away. Or else I'll blast everyone in the chawl with my gun.

Savita ran out before Jeevanlal finished his sentence.

Jeevanlal adjusted his safi around his waist and opened the cupboard. He took out the revolver from the vault, loaded it with three bullets and started for Manilal's house.

In the corridor he met Savita – pale and panting.

He grabbed her by her shoulders, Got it?

Savita shook her head and said, Sharadee had a bath, Manilal had a bath, Deepak had a bath, and finally Tommy had a bath. The game's over and the soap's gone. How can Sharada return a soap that no longer exists?

Savita gave a wan smile in an attempt to placate Jeevanlal.

Jeevanlal's anger shot up when he saw that smile. Burning with rage, he resolved that those bastards' time had run out. Maniya and Sharadee deserved to be shot dead. Savli is plain

stupid. Why does she have to run and tell Sharada every time she farts? The stupid sentimental slob lends out my brand new phoren soap and Maniya ends up rubbing it on his thighs! What did she get by showing off to Sharada? I won't stand with folded hands and watch the motherfucker rob me of my scented soap.

Jeevanlal reached Manilal's house mumbling to himself. Through the living room window he saw Manilal sitting at the low table eating sakkarpara.

Fuming with rage, Jeevanlal muttered, The old baldy doesn't have ten hairs left on his head, yet he puffs them up and sits down to a breakfast of tea and sakkarpara! My name is not Jeevanlal if I don't gun down his entire family.

As he stood swearing quietly, Tommy rested his front paws on Jeevanlal's safi and wagged his tail. Forced into tactical retreat, Jeevanlal bumped into Savita who was following him. The gun fell from his hand. Jeevanlal bent down to pick it up.

Through the window grill, Manilal saw Jeevanlal rise gun in hand and said, Oi, Jeevanlal, you seem all set for shikar this morning. Or are you rehearsing for some office play?

Jeevanlal thundered in his heart, Your father must be rehearsing for some office play. You swine, I'll finish you. Think of sakkarpara when I shoot all your family in their shins and you have to watch them all limp.

Savita spoke up, He has come to ask about the soap.

With a gun in his hand?

That's his sense of humour.

Really?

Sure, he'll brandish a gun at me even if I forget mustard in the seasoning.

Manilal wouldn't notice even if there's too much salt in his food, said Sharada and went into the kitchen. She returned with a plate of sakkarpara and a cup of tea and invited Jeevanlal to the table. Have some tea and sakkarpara, she said.

As she bent down to place the cup of tea on the table, Jeevanlal caught a glimpse of her breasts, about the size of two little Tommys. He got angrier looking at the valley between her breasts. What a vamp! Though she is about to die, she doesn't forget to thrust her bosom about. At half past seven in the morning what he needed was his soap, not a pair of breasts. Now he'd better be on guard. He won't be able to raise the gun if he put even a single sakkarpara in his mouth.

But Sharada coaxed him, You must have at least two.

As Sharada bent once again to serve the sakkarpara, Jeevanlal thought she was talking about her breasts and wondered how breasts could be eaten.

Listlessly, he put the gun aside to pick up the sakkarpara which found its way to his mouth. When he took a sip of the tea, Sharada gathered the folds of her sari, sat down beside him and said, Bhai, your phoren soap was just wonderful! What fragrance it had! The whole house was filled with its aroma!

Annoyed, Jeevanlal bellowed, So, where is it?

Sharada said moodily, You know what happened. Still you ask for it?

Manilal nodded in approval, We, too, want the soap.

Jeevanlal screamed, So, then, where's it gone?

Sharada explained while serving another helping of sakkarpara. First I had a bath with three buckets of water. Then Manilal bathed with two, Deepak with one, and the remaining half bucketful was used for Tommy's bath. Everyone rubbed the soap so hard, it no longer exists on earth.

Manilal continued to praise the soap, So damn' good, you want to bathe all day.

Jeevanlal finished the plate of sakkarpara. Upon Sharada and Manilal's insistence, he had another cup of tea and returned home.

He put the gun back into the vault of his cupboard, sat on the chair and started thinking.

When Savita saw him sitting with a long face, she remarked, How can we control destiny with our puny little hands? What the One With A Thousand Hands does, must be good for us, isn't it? Accept His judgement. Leave everything to Him. Can you get the soap back by worrying about it?

But Jeevanlal was perturbed. He was consumed with the

thought, I am a lowly creature. What difference did it make whether I, Sharada or Manilal used the soap? Blinded by greed and delusion, I was about to take their lives. There is no end to my bad karma.

Raising his head, he spoke, Savita, my soul won't find peace till I've atoned for my sins.

Your repentance is atonement enough. Savita tried to alleviate his guilt.

You forgive me because you are my wife, but I am guilty before God. I must punish myself.

A cup of hot milk will make you feel better.

Feel better, my foot! For me it's a matter of life and death, and you can only think of milk!

Or else, shall I give you methi-na-khakhra and chhundo?

Jeevanlal stared at Savita. He made an angry gesture with his hands. Savita went to the kitchen. When she returned with two khakhras and chhundo in a plate, Jeevanlal had put on his dhoti, kurta and topi and was about to leave the house.

Savita shouted after him, Don't you want a bath? Once food is mentioned, how can you leave the house without eating?

Jeevanlal disappeared down the stairs without a word.

Down the lane was a small park. On a wooden bench there, he sat and held his head in his hands. His eyes became moist as he contemplated his predicament.

Finally, he wiped the tears with his kurta and started for home. He had made his resolve.

When he crossed the threshold, he called out with emotion, Savita, O Savita.

Savita was angry, Where did you go?

I'll walk on all fours till my heart is purified.

What do you mean?

I will not walk on my two feet till my soul is completely purged of the longing for phoren soap. That is my vow.

Why say such harsh words?

Sins must be atoned for.

From then on, wherever Jeevanlal went, he went on all fours.

At night, he slept on all fours like a horse. If he ever lost balance in his sleep and fell on the bed, he fasted for two days without a drop of water.

Sometimes his dhoti would get torn while travelling on all fours to his office. So he decided to wear a kurta and shorts for going out.

On the way back from the office, he would climb the stairs on all fours. Tommy invariably barked on seeing him.

At times, Jeevanlal would get wild and mutter, You bastard, go bark at your father! Get lost, go bark at Deepak and Maniya. Then, with a peaceful mind, he would climb the

stairs slowly on all fours and reach home.

For the chawl children, this was great entertainment. Every evening, they would line up on the staircase and wait for him to return home. As soon as he entered the chawl, they would start yelling. When he reached the landing, they would start showering breads of all kinds on him – rotli, dhebra and bhakhri. And when Jeevanlal barked at them, "Bow-wow!" the children loved it. They would not leave him in peace till he reached home.

Wearing white shorts and a vest, Jeevanlal would settle down in his special place in a corner under the table.

Jeevanlal would think that the world of the four-legged is different from that of the two-legged. When your head is low, your nostrils get filled with dust, mud, pebbles and the stench of drains. Your limbs are coated with filth if you have to wade through cow dung, sheep pellets and dog shit.

Then his nephew returned from Abu Dhabi to get married. Everything was arranged in a week. There was no way they could avoid going to his wedding. Jeevanlal was persuaded to wear a long silk kurta over his shorts before he settled on the back seat of the taxicab on all fours. Savita sat next to the cab driver, on the front seat.

But the driver refused to start the cab, I don't carry animals in this vehicle.

/50

Savita explained, But this is a human being.

The driver was conservative, Human beings walk on two feet.

Savita gave her excuse, He has polio. The doctor has advised him to walk on all fours.

The driver made incomprehensible comments about the state of the medical profession today and started the cab.

The wedding reception was aglow with the light of thousands of little red and yellow electric bulbs.

There was a buffet dinner. Savita filled Jeevanlal's plate and placed it on the ground. Jeevanlal started with poori and potato curry. Suddenly a black dog put its muzzle in the plate and helped itself to rice and kadhi. Jeevanlal pushed Blackie away. But Blackie bared its fangs at him. Jeevanlal started barking at the dog, and bit Blackie on its back. Blackie ran away.

The dining public gathered around Jeevanlal in a circle. Plates were abandoned by the crowd to give Jeevanlal a standing ovation.

When Savita heard the applause, she came running and asked, What happened?

Someone from the crowd said, Jeevanlal bit a dog.

Why?

Jeevanlal tried to defend himself, The dog was eating from my plate.

Leave that plate. I'll get you another, said Savita. She served him another plate and left to mingle with her friends.

Jeevanlal mixed rice, kadhi and potatoes once again. But before he could start eating, Blackie returned with a gang of four other dogs. The five dogs attacked his plate together. Before Jeevanlal could save his plate, the kadhi was wiped out by long tongues, the rice mixture disappeared and the potatoes vanished into thin air.

Jeevanlal could do nothing but gnash his teeth.

Later that night Jeevanlal brooded that there were impediments even on the path of penance. Now even dogs interfered with his life.

He tried to sleep on all fours as usual, but could not fall asleep. He thought, Damn it, what a life! I feel like dying. And all this mess for a cake of soap! I've been betrayed by my very own. Savita's love for me has evaporated. Now she only performs wifely duties. And Sharada! She, who brushes herself against me at the slightest pretext! The flirt, she unbuttons her blouse and puffs up her balloons again and again! But what about me? I slogged all my life to give Savita a better life, and it turns out she couldn't even look after a bar of soap for me! She gave away my phoren soap to rub in Maniya's armpits. Everyone has conspired against me! Why else would Deepak laugh at me? Even Tommy barks at me when I climb the stairs. The chawl kids throw stale dhebra at me. As if I were a beggar! How have I harmed them? I just don't understand this damned world. There is no choice but to end my life.

Undaunted by the darkness, Jeevanlal went on all fours to the same park where he had taken the vow of atonement.

There he saw a sadhu sitting on a bench, sobbing copiously.

Jeevanlal forgot his problems and leapt onto the bench, next to the sadhu.

When he saw Jeevanlal, the sadhu stopped sobbing.

Jeevanlal asked, O Sadhu Maharaj, what profound unhappiness in your life causes you to grieve in the wilderness? Unhappiness is the domain of rooted householders like me. A sadhu is always on the move.

The sadhu began, Ever since I was young, I was inclined to meditation. I lived with my parents and sister in a small town. I had no interest in studies so I used to write Ram-nam on my slate all the time. My teacher used to say this boy will be a sadhu some day. My parents were glad. I left home when I was twenty. I served an old sadhu with utmost devotion. He gave me a mantra. I went to the Himalayas to chant the mantra. I sat in a cave and meditated on the mantra. All went well for about a month.

Jeevanlal asked excitedly, So, did you see God?

Not quite, but my mind had achieved the single-mindedness

/150

necessary for it. But trouble started before I could achieve realization.

You mean ...

The sadhu continued the story. I saw my mother's face. I saw her puffing to ignite the firewood in the choolah. Then I saw a pot of boiling kadhi. My mind was possessed by the thought of kadhi. Crackling fried cumin and finely chopped fresh ginger floating on top! Oh, the lip smacking taste of curds mixed with besan! That did it. After that whenever I closed my eyes for meditation, I saw steaming pots of kadhi. God became redundant, I yearned for kadhi.

Jeevanlal could appreciate the problem. In a Himalayan cave, you could not have found curds. Also, how could you get cumin and ginger there?

So I returned home. My mother was speechless on seeing me. My father and sister were also shocked. Mother asked me, Beta, why are you back? You had gone to seek God! Have you found Him? I confessed, That's true, Ma! But what can I do? When I meditate upon Him, I can only remember your kadhi. God slips away easily from my mind, but your kadhi cannot be forgotten. From that day on, Ma cooked kadhi every morning, noon and evening. For a month I had nothing but kadhi. A stage came when I'd become nauseated at the sight of it. Yet I admonished myself, Here's kadhi. Have some more!

Jeevanlal understood the moral of the story, Is this how

you freed yourself from the bondage of desire?

The story doesn't end here. I went to the Himalayas once again. This time kadhi was not on my mind. I started chanting the mantra. But after a fortnight, the vision of kadhi returned. The same simmering pots were floating before my eyes. It was as if God had abandoned me. Whether I kept my eyes open or closed, I could see only kadhi, kadhi and more kadhi. Then I would feel nauseous and retch and feel as if I was dying. Finally, I got fed up. What was the point in living if there was no hope of finding God? As I sat on the bench here, I was overcome by these thoughts.

Jeevanlal's eyes were moist with compassion, My lot is a little better than yours. The soap that floats before my eyes at least has a pleasant fragrance. You have found yourself in pure hell.

The sadhu moved closer to him and wiped Jeevanlal's tears.

Suddenly it was dawn.

The two of them sat together on the garden bench overwhelmed by the sight of sunrise over the squalid city. The copper sunlight touched every little corner of the city, even the dog shit.

The sadhu whispered the mantra in Jeevanlal's ear.

Nothing more remained to be said.

Jeevanlal sprang up from the bench bolt upright. He bent to touch his toes a couple of times and walked out of the park.

Jeevanlal carried a bagful of the phoren soap with him when he knocked on the main door of his house. He roared, Savli, O my Savli!

Wiping her hands with a corner of her sari, Savita opened the door. She was relieved to see him on his feet and said, I'm fortunate. I had just planned to stitch curtains from all your dhotis.

But Jeevanlal was hardly in a mood to appreciate her attempts at frugality. He said, Just see what I've got here!

Savita noticed the plastic bag and asked, What is it?

Jeevanlal proudly said. Phoren soap.

So many!

Have I not served my firm diligently for years? My application for a loan of five thousand rupees and one month's leave was granted without a murmur, in five minutes. Now what other business do I have – morning, noon and evening? Jeevanlal moved closer to Savita and whispered, The foam makes you feel as if you are bathing in the ocean surf!

It's already ten o'clock. You haven't had a thing to eat since morning. I'll fix some batata pauva.

First, get me some hot water. I want to have a bath.

When Savita returned from the kitchen, she saw Jeevanlal squatting on the floor of the living room, busy arranging the soap bars like the coaches of a train. Savita joined him in making the soap-train. The train encircled their living room.

Savita ran back to the kitchen when she heard the water boil. Jeevanlal lifted the first bar from the train, delicately removed its wrapper and kept it aside. He then removed the translucent butter paper around the bar, held it close to his nose, inhaled deeply and gave it to Savita. Savita closed her eyes and inhaled the fragrance. Jeevanlal's hands now held the shiny, pink, naked bar. He breathed deep on its aroma.

Savita said, The safi is on the peg in the bathroom.

Jeevanlal entered the bathroom humming a tune from an old Hindi film.

He emerged after an hour.

He saw that there was a plate of batata pauva on the table and Savita was fast asleep on the mat surrounded by the soap-train.

"Phoren Soap" was first published as a limited bilingual edition in English and Gujarati in *Phoren Soap*, 1997.

MAUJILA MANILAL

Characters

SAVITA. *40. A diligent, middle class housewife*

SHARMISHTHA. *36. Housewife.* SAVITA'*s neighbour and friend.*

MANILAL. *55 and a bachelor.*

JAGDEEP. *24. Orphan,* SAVITA'*s neighbour and lover.*

RANCHOD. *45.* SAVITA'*s husband. He is a clerk with an old fashioned Gujarati accountant.*

NAVNEET. *45.* SHARMISHTHA'*s husband and* RANCHOD'*s friend. Part-time accountant.*

YAMRAJ. 22. *The God of Death, a player of dice.*

VISHNU. 8. *Lord of the Universe and* YAMRAJ'*s competitor at dice.*

SAVITA's house. A room opening out to a chawl. The passage of the chawl is visible from the door and window. Visible in the room is a cot and a chowkdi, the bounded off space with a tap used for cleaning vessels or clothes.

SHARMISHTHA's house. Same as SAVITA's, only it has a phone.

The passage of the chawl. Visible from both the houses.

JAGDEEP's room. A narrow, untidy bachelor's room. Several wires are strung up pell-mell across the room. Old clothes are hanging from the wires, along with several negatives. On a table is a stack of photographs and some photography equipment.

Hell. Empty space.

ACT I

SCENE I

Darkness.

RANCHOD'*s voice in a monotonous chant.* He wooed sixteen thousand gopis, yet Krishna was a Bal Brahmachari. Draupadi, lone wife of five Pandavas, was revered as a sati. But Rama, Rama of the ekapatni vrata, Rama is the Man amongst men, Maryada Purshottam.

This is Kaliyug, dark, depraved Kaliyug that changes man and beast. Kali has the reins in his hands and all the virtuous men of Satyug have vanished. Pleasure, pleasure, pleasure is the all of life. God forgotten, who cares about life after death in Kaliyug, who recognizes Shiva.

Want to save yourself from the dangers of Kaliyug? Think God with all your might, worship him, immerse yourself in him through constant, ardent japa. Try it just once and miracle of miracles! Down will come Vishnu in his Pushpak Viman to take you, forgetting Lakshmi who sits massaging his feet, saying, My devotee is desperate for me. Prabhu will carry you off and he'll pound at the gates of Swarg for you. He'll walk you through it, revealing all its glories. You'll see the apsaras dance, the kinnaras sing, and behold the rajhans of Swarg feeding on pearls!

But then your life has to be untarnished, pure and spotless as a newborn flower, inspire family and caste brethren. Come then, increase their knowledge, do tilanjali for your self-centred, lustful life. Come let's build lives that shine, pure and holy. Let's build our Ramrajya.

SCENE 2

Light. SAVITA*'s house.* SAVITA *and* SHARMISHTHA *are making pickles, in everyday, ordinary saris.*

SAVITA *(looking once again at the clock).* This clock has stopped. What *is* the time?

SHARMISHTHA. You've asked this twenty two times in the past fifteen minutes. (*Imitating* SAVITA.) What's the time, what's the time? I'm sick of it. If your clock is slow, for heaven's sake get it repaired. Or, do you think I turned back the needle when I came in?

SAVITA. What should I do?

SHARMISHTHA. That's it! I don't want to make pickles with you any more.

SAVITA. Why?

SHARMISHTHA. I ruined my afternoon nap to make pickles. Not to listen to your silly blabber.

SAVITA. A whole day! I can't live one whole day without him.

SHARMISHTHA. If that's how you feel, why in heaven's name did you marry Ranchodbhai?

SAVITA. What happiness has he given me as a husband?

SHARMISHTHA. Naseeb! What fate decrees, we bear.

SAVITA. Why didn't he turn up yesterday?

SHARMISHTHA. God knows. I saw him sitting on the steps.

SAVITA. Who?

SHARMISHTHA. The one you await so eagerly.

SAVITA. *He* was sitting on the steps? What was he doing there?

SHARMISHTHA. Listening to the cricket commentary.

SAVITA. Fool, fool, *fool*! Who *are* you talking about?

SHARMISHTHA. Jagdeep. Your lover!

SAVITA. Just because I snatched a few kisses with him some years ago? You call that love?

SHARMISHTHA. Liar. You're dying to meet him. You plead with

him. Come up, come up here! And what about last year? Didn't you set me up for sentry duty.

SAVITA. Oh yes! And your bhai? Remember how he suddenly showed up! And was he surprised. What are you doing here, standing outside, he asked you.

SHARMISHTHA (*smiling fondly*). Poor Ranchodbhai. He's such a simpleton. I lied through my teeth and took him home. Luckily there was nobody there. And I had some leftovers from breakfast.

SAVITA (*looks at the clock*). This clock has definitely stopped.

SHARMISHTHA. Savita, look here. You're married to Ranchodbhai. Sure, he's not the best looking man around, but he, after all, belongs to a good family. He doesn't touch liquor or other women. What more do you want? Why spoil the family honour?

SAVITA. Loving someone has nothing to do with family honour. I've loved men since I was a child. Why, even in the Ninth Standard I was in love with three boys.

SHARMISHTHA. I had only one lover. But he didn't touch me even once.

SAVITA. What's so great about that? I had at least two lovers in each standard.

SHARMISHTHA. Didn't people talk?

SAVITA. They did, but behind my back. Everybody wanted to be friends with me, you see.

SHARMISHTHA. How things change with marriage. Married women are pure, pristine. And faithful.

Both are lost in thought for a moment. They continue making pickles.

SAVITA. I've spent half my life with him. And not a single child to show for so many years.

SHARMISHTHA. And what do you think *I* have done? Had the five Pandavas?

SAVITA. This house is so empty. This yawning emptiness will eat me up.

SHARMISHTHA. Why didn't you join sewing classes with me?

SAVITA. This treacherous heart of mine, there's a hole drilled right through it.

SHARMISHTHA. Oh, come on. Why torture yourself?

SAVITA. When you were pushing silken thread through little buttons and working at your zigzag embroidery a stranger was teaching me the lessons of love!

SHARMISHTHA. You don't mean Jagdeep, do you, even then?

SAVITA. Forget Jagdeep! A parrot has flown away with my heart in his beak.

SHARMISHTHA. Does Ranchodbhai know?

SAVITA. Who knows? All he needs is that pious religious magazine, *Jankalyan*.

SHARMISHTHA. You dropped Jagdeep like a hot potato. That was wrong.

SAVITA. Oh, he's callow. He'll forget.

SHARMISHTHA. Love is for life.

SAVITA. Come, come, why do you always take his side? Do you like him?

SHARMISHTHA. What are you saying?

SAVITA. You won't even admit to yourself ...

SHARMISHTHA. Are you out of your mind?

SAVITA. Are you telling me you never called him to your house?

SHARMISHTHA. No. I did. When there were phone calls for him. He hung around afterwards. That's all there is to it. And of course, he talked only of you.

SAVITA. And you wanted him to talk of you?

SHARMISHTHA. I'm not like you, you two-timer! Once married, you can't go around falling in love.

SAVITA (*lifts the pot of pickles and glances at the clock*). What's the time?

SHARMISHTHA. Who *is* this upstart who's got a string around you. I can bet he's only pretending to be in love with you.

SAVITA. So? Even false lovers are rare these days.

SHARMISHTHA. What about Jagdeep?

SAVITA. Him! He has a problem. Like me. Trapped in true love.

SHARMISHTHA. *Who* is this, this man who has trapped you in true love?

SAVITA. Manilal!

SHARMISHTHA. Manilal?

SAVITA. Yes Manilal! Oh, isn't it the most pleasurable name you've ever heard?

SHARMISHTHA. Oh? When did you meet this Manilal?

SAVITA. That memorable first meeting! I remember it so well. Remember my sister-in-law's son's accident.

SHARMISHTHA. The one who died fifteen days after the accident?

SAVITA. Yes, the same. Your bhai and I had gone to Parel to see him at the hospital. Manilal was admitted in the same room. He kept staring at me. And me, my eyes couldn't get their fill of him. And ... a swirl of light churned in my stomach.

SHARMISHTHA. Then? You aren't telling me what Manilal did! Very cunning. Come on, tell!

SAVITA. I don't have to conceal anything from you, do I? I went every afternoon for hospital visits. To see the boy, you know. Manilal would drop me back in a taxi.

SHARMISHTHA. Ja, ja! In a taxi?

SAVITA. Yes. He would curl his fingers round mine. And never utter a word.

SHARMISHTHA. Really?

SAVITA. My heart thumped hard. My feet floated above the earth.

SHARMISHTHA. Then?

SAVITA. Then? Then Manilal would come home. He'd have tea. He'd make love to me. Manilal! My Manilal!

SHARMISHTHA. What does he look like?

SAVITA. Oh, just one look. That's all you need. When he talks a restless desire surges through my body. His personality is like a foaming ocean, his voice a flute. And his laughter! The ultimate happiness! When he removes his black cap and hangs it on the hook! Oh! Even apsaras are denied the pleasure of running their fingers through his grey hair and inhaling the fragrance of brahmi oil.

SHARMISHTHA. Will you please speak a language I can understand? How does he look?

SAVITA. Like the green after the rains, the mischief of Holi, like the crops fluttering in the fields, the table fan whirring.

SHARMISHTHA. You are menopausal! Whoever heard of love at this age! All you need now is to commit suicide.

SAVITA. Hé Vayumandal! Supreme amongst the Devas, explain to this naive pativrata. Open her eyes to the love of another man. Explain to her the pleasure of dependence on another man! This woman whose world is bound by the lanes of Bhuleshwar, this silly old chawl. Explain to this idiot who thinks her husband is her Parameshwar. Do this foolish woman some good!

MANILAL *enters. He wears a dhoti, half coat, black cap, black shoes and red socks. He tiptoes in and covers* SAVITA*'s eyes with both his hands.* SHARMISHTHA *watches with eyes wide open.*

SAVITA. Who, who is it? Oh! It's you!

MANILAL *and* SAVITA *gaze at each other.* SHARMISHTHA *lowers her head and leaves.*

MANILAL. Who was that? That cultured lady, who left without as much as a glance at me?

SAVITA. That was Sharmishtha.

MANILAL. Ah, so this is the sundari you've talked to me about so often.

SAVITA. Oh, why did you leave me like that? Just one day and that was longer than a whole yug.

MANILAL. I suffered too. Your absence was unbearable.

SAVITA. I waited and waited for you, counting each second. My eyes drooped with exhausted anticipation. Yet, you didn't come.

MANILAL (*sings*). I was impatient to meet you, sanam/I spent the night thinking of you, sanam.

SAVITA. What power had you in its grip, keeping you away from me? See the beads of this armlet have faded, washed by my tears. I spent the night with my head on it, tears streaming down, thinking of you ...

MANILAL (*sings*). Suffer what Jagannath imposes on you/That which your lover loves/Expend more love on it.

SAVITA. Without you all roads lead to a dark vacuum.

MANILAL. Separation only for a day. And you seem so anaemic ... but didn't I tell you?

SAVITA. What?

MANILAL. Have you forgotten? The work?

SAVITA. The heart doesn't remember any work.

MANILAL. The heart remembers only work, not talk.

SAVITA. What talk?

MANILAL. Our talk.

SAVITA. I remember all our talk about love.

MANILAL. What did I tell you when we parted day before yesterday?

SAVITA. What?

MANILAL. A white fairy ...

SAVITA. Like a white fairy ...

MANILAL. A fairy, an Ambassador? Have you forgotten?

SAVITA. How can I forget that?

MANILAL (*teasing*). And how does it arrive?

SAVITA. On four wheels!

MANILAL. No, with money! I'd gone to the showroom, saw the car, deposited the amount and got the receipt ...

SAVITA. By then it was six in the evening, your deadline to reach my house?

MANILAL. Kashmir! Wouldn't you like to go there?

SAVITA. Kashmir? In a white Ambassador car?

MANILAL *takes out a string of mogra flowers from his pocket.*

SAVITA. Oh, my heart ...

SHARMISHTHA *enters. She stands at the threshold.*

SHARMISHTHA. You left this bowl and spoon at my place

yesterday. I've come to return it. (*She comes in, keeps the bowl and spoon down and moves towards the chowkdi.*)

SAVITA. Sharmishtha, have you met Manilal?

MANILAL (*to* SAVITA). I entered the house and she floated away like a wave.

SHARMISHTHA (*to* SAVITA). I came to return the bowl and spoon. I would've forgotten all about it otherwise. Well, I'd better leave now.

SAVITA. Why don't you sit down?

MANILAL (*to* SHARMISHTHA). Please sit!

SHARMISHTHA (*to* SAVITA). No, no. I've lots of work.

MANILAL. And you think we don't?

SHARMISHTHA. Ask Savita!

SAVITA. What work? Manilal doesn't seek permission to put himself to work.

MANILAL (*to* SHARMISHTHA). You're very busy?

SHARMISHTHA. Yes, yes. I've a lot of work.

SHARMISHTHA *slips out.* SAVITA *bolts the door, and goes to* MANILAL.

MANILAL (*putting the string of mogras in her hair*). Live a chaste life free of lust, stigma and sin, just like these mogras.

SAVITA. Manilal, my Manilal. My body is afire with indescribable passion.

MANILAL. This hungry heart burns at the heavenly scent of your hair. You've seeped into every cell of my being.

SAVITA. Then do it one more time!

MANILAL. What?

SAVITA. Woo me. In English. With your special, poetic rhythms.

MANILAL. The God of Love has blessed you.

SAVITA. You are my teacher. Do it!

MANILAL. What?

SAVITA. Love me! Woo me with your English poetry! One more time! Do it!

MANILAL. You want the same poem?

SAVITA. Yes. The same. Still the earth once again with your song of love/Let the verse of love spill over/Each line overflows with the melody of your love/Let it overflow/ Embrace me with your touch rhythm/Transport me into ecstasy with your love/Let me drown in your love. One more time, just once I want to hear your priceless poetry.

There is a knock on the door. SAVITA *opens it.* SHARMISHTHA *enters.* MANILAL *listens to the conversation between the two with interest.*

SHARMISHTHA. You bolted the door from inside?

SAVITA. Yes.

SHARMISHTHA. You have a white sari, don't you?

SAVITA. I have *two* white saris.

SHARMISHTHA. The organdy.

SAVITA. Yes?

SHARMISHTHA. I want to see the colour of that sari.

SAVITA. You want to see the colour of a white sari! Why?

SHARMISHTHA. I want to buy a sari of the same colour.

SAVITA. Right now?

SHARMISHTHA. Well, if you're not too busy ... I'd like to take it now.

SAVITA. Come in and take it.

SHARMISHTHA. I'll return it immediately.

SAVITA. No, no. I don't need it right now. Return it later.

SHARMISHTHA *leaves.* SAVITA *leaves the door ajar and goes towards* MANILAL.

SAVITA. Remember the first day of love?

MANILAL. It was a day like this.

SAVITA. I remember it too!

MANILAL. Your head on my chest.

SAVITA. My mad heart beats the same way even today!

MANILAL. My sweet Savita, come closer to me.

SAVITA. Cling to me. Let not even a lotus stem come between us.

MANILAL. Savita!

SAVITA. My Manilal!

SHARMISHTHA *suddenly opens the door and enters.* MANILAL *and* SAVITA *fall apart.*

SHARMISHTHA. May I come in?

SAVITA. Why, what is it now?

SHARMISHTHA. Phone call. For you.

SAVITA. Now?

SHARMISHTHA. Yes, now.

MANILAL *stares at them.*

SAVITA. Who is it?

SHARMISHTHA. How would I know? Here, take your sari.

SAVITA. You are through with it?

SHARMISHTHA. Yes. I'll put it in your cupboard.

SHARMISHTHA *goes towards the closet.* SAVITA *goes towards her.*

SAVITA (*whispers*). You make a cup of tea for Manilal while I answer the phone.

SHARMISHTHA (*whispers*). Alone with him? Look, my sari's so filthy.

SAVITA (*whispers*). He's like a family member. It doesn't matter. (*Louder.*) Two spoons of sugar. (*Slowly turning towards* MANILAL.) I'll answer the phone and come ... immediately.

MANILAL. Take your time ...

SAVITA *goes out.*

MANILAL. What a mature, cultured, arya woman Savita is!

SHARMISHTHA. She's like an elder sister to me.

MANILAL. You and I have only just met. But she does not tire of praising you!

SHARMISHTHA. Lies!

MANILAL. I swear by you!

SHARMISHTHA. You swear? *You* are a liar then. Should I add masala?

MANILAL. Where?

SHARMISHTHA. In the tea?

MANILAL. Pahh, tea!

SHARMISHTHA. Don't you want tea?

MANILAL. I do. I want!

SHARMISHTHA. Masala tea?

MANILAL. No, green.

SHARMISHTHA. I don't want any tongue-twisting tangles with you. Talk straight, will you. Do you want tea or don't you?

MANILAL. Who wants tea?

SHARMISHTHA. Tchhhh! Why were you silent when I put the water on? What a waste of time! I shouldn't have stayed back.

MANILAL. Yes, but we've some work to do, don't we?

SHARMISHTHA. What work?

MANILAL. Look at me once.

SHARMISHTHA. What's there in your old face?

MANILAL. You'll never know if you don't look at me.

SHARMISHTHA. What's there to know? You're just an old man.

MANILAL. Look deep into my eyes and then say that.

SHARMISHTHA. What, what do you want me to say?

MANILAL. Whatever you want. But first look into my eyes.

SHARMISHTHA. What?

MANILAL. Your heart is made of stone!

SHARMISHTHA. I'm a pativrata and Navneetlal is my ...

MANILAL. Navneetlal? Who's that?

SHARMISHTHA. My husband.

MANILAL. Oh. But why are you at such a loss? Come, sit here peacefully.

SHARMISHTHA. It's wrong to sit alone with a stranger.

MANILAL. Why? What do you think will happen?

SHARMISHTHA. Don't you have an ounce of shame?

MANILAL. What shame? Does anyone know? Just forget Navneetlal for a while.

SHARMISHTHA. What! Forget him and run after you? For a woman her husband is her bhagwan.

MANILAL. When did I deny that?

SHARMISHTHA. You don't want to get into any kind of an affair do you?

MANILAL. Why? Are you afraid?

SHARMISHTHA. Afraid of what?

MANILAL. Of love! (*takes out a string of roses from his pocket.*) Here, I've brought something for you.

SHARMISHTHA. Like the one I saw in Savita's hair?

MANILAL. No, these are roses. Look at them! Red, red roses. Let me put them on your hair, please.

SHARMISHTHA (*by rote*). Spoil the daal and the day is ruined/ Spoil the pickle and the year is ruined/Spoil a woman and life itself is ruined.

MANILAL. Once! Just once! After that, if you don't like it, throw it away. May I?

SHARMISHTHA (*coyly*). All right. But you're not to touch me!

MANILAL. Only your hair, that's all.

MANILAL *puts the roses on her hair and touches her.*

SHARMISHTHA (*with a start*). I told you not to! Why did you touch me?

MANILAL. You liked it?

SHARMISHTHA. Behave yourself! Your lover Savita will soon be here.

MANILAL. I want you.

SHARMISHTHA. Listen to him! Hardly knows me and he wants me! I'm not Savita.

MANILAL. Ah, the meeting of thc eyes!

SHARMISHTHA. What's that?

MANILAL. Touch!

SHARMISHTHA. Behave yourself, will you?

MANILAL. You in my arms ...

SHARMISHTHA. Don't talk to me like that.

MANILAL. Then sing a song.

SHARMISHTHA. Why should I?

MANILAL. Savita praises your voice.

SHARMISHTHA. Really?

MANILAL. I swear by you.

SHARMISHTHA. You swear? You're such a liar.

MANILAL. Promise, I won't touch you.

SHARMISHTHA. Liar!

MANILAL. I'll sit here and listen.

SHARMISHTHA. You do that ... or else! (SHARMISHTHA *sits on the floor, closes her eyes and recites a poem tunelessly.* MANILAL *sits on the cot and listens.*) O God! We worship you/Lofty is your name/We sing your praise daily/Let our work be done/ Bring laughter into our lives/Keep our hearts clean. (SAVITA *enters.* SHARMISHTHA *continues singing with her eyes closed.*) Oh God! Forgive us if we trespass.

MANILAL. What a cultured, understanding, arya woman.

SAVITA. Sharmishtha has the capacity to uphold a woman's dharma. She's full of it. She wants to live an unblemished life. Isn't that right, Sharmishtha?

SHARMISHTHA *gets up to leave.*

SAVITA *(stops* her *near the door and asks her softly.)* So, did you like my Manilal?

SHARMISHTHA (*softly*). Loafer!

SAVITA (*softly*). Very pretty roses.

SHARMISHTHA (*louder*). I'm leaving. Your bhai will be getting back.

SHARMISHTHA *leaves.* SAVITA *bolts the door. She draws the curtains. It gets dark.*

SAVITA. Manilal! This body is melting. I'm drunk with your love.

MANILAL. Savita, my Savita! My arms await your body.

SAVITA. You are enchanting. You've seduced me with your poetry.

MANILAL. Do you want me to do it again?

SAVITA. Yes! I want to savour your poetry.

MANILAL. Then here it is. (MANILAL's *chant is full of mispronounciations and is off tune. Both try to dance to the poem.*) I had a little pony/Whose name was Dapple Grey/I lent him to a lady/To ride a mile away/She whipped him/ And she lashed him/She rode him/Through the mire/I would not lend/My pony now/For all the lady's ire.

SAVITA. Words dispersed in ten directions, spreading the nectar of life. Love had been reduced to ashes, emotions had been crushed. A lifeless body and deadened sensitivities are revived. The earth is rendered speechless with these words, and the love that has burst forth has wrought magic. Every throbbing heart, every vanquished mind is now at peace. And I ... every part of my being is illuminated with the fire of love, I am awash with it. Every cell of my being is burning with a volcanic love, it soothes the heart. How come he doesn't know these things?

MANILAL. Why don't you teach him?

SAVITA. He's not interested in women. (*Suddenly there are flashes of light.*) Lightning! (*She is thrilled and begins to hum.*) Lightning flashes in the sky/The rain patters down/...

MANILAL. Come closer.

SAVITA (*romantically*). I'm frightened.

MANILAL *and* SAVITA *take each other into their arms.*

MANILAL. Closer, come closer.

There is a flash of light again.

SAVITA. Lightning has no sound.

MANILAL. But light has wings.

SAVITA. There's light everywhere.

MANILAL. For a moment darkness has melted.

A flash of light appears again.

SAVITA. The doors are open!

MANILAL. But you had closed them!

SAVITA. Somebody is taking photographs.

MANILAL. Without asking?

SAVITA *lifts the curtains. Again there is light.* JAGDEEP *can be seen. He wears tight jeans, a printed shirt and white sports shoes. He has a camera with a flashgun in his hand and a cassette recorder on his shoulder.*

SAVITA (*screams*). Jagdeep!

MANILAL (*in a collected voice*). Namaste.

SAVITA (*irritated*). I told you not to come before five o'clock.

JAGDEEP (*in the manner of a Hindi villain*). I want to blackmail you!

SAVITA (*screams*). By taking photographs?

JAGDEEP. Yes! I'll expose you to Ranchoduncle.

JAGDEEP *takes two or three photographs of the two in rapid succession.*

MANILAL (*in perfect control*). This is the cricketer, isn't it?

SAVITA. Yes. (*Calm now, she turns to* MANILAL.) Come closer.

MANILAL. Let me wear my cap.

SAVITA. Cling to me like jellyfish, drape me around like a wet sari.

MANILAL (*puts on the cap and poses for the photograph*). Is this the same man who dropped four catches in the match against your neighbour?

JAGDEEP (*taking a photograph, enraged*). Yes, I'm the same Jagdeep. She used to drag me away from cricket matches.

MANILAL. Why?

JAGDEEP. To teach me lessons of love.

MANILAL. Jagdeepbhai, we shouldn't use such words for a chaste woman.

JAGDEEP. Don't act too smart. You're the cause of this explosion.

SAVITA. Mind your tongue. He's elder to you.

JAGDEEP. He has made a bonfire of my life. I'll give a copy of all these photographs to Ranchoduncle.

SAVITA. You won't give me any?

MANILAL. Jagdeepbhai, give me two copies of each. I'll bear the cost.

SAVITA. If you wanted to blackmail me, you should've told me! I would've worn a nice sari!

JAGDEEP (*taken aback*). You mean, you *want* to be blackmailed?

MANILAL *prepares to go.*

SAVITA. Why are you off?

MANILAL. It's five o'clock. Time to go. Jagdeepbhai, don't forget the photographs. (*To* SAVITA.) Avjo.

JAGDEEP (*parroting him*). Avjo.

MANILAL (*to* JAGDEEP). Avjo.

SAVITA. Avjo.

MANILAL. I'll definitely come.

MANILAL *leaves.*

JAGDEEP. Has the old man left?

SAVITA. Didn't you see? He's not a thief like you to come in the dark.

JAGDEEP. I have the key you'd given me. (*In Hindi.*) SAVITA, meri jaan! That man is the very devil! Forget him. I'm the only one who loves you. Come close to me. Give me a kiss.

SAVITA. Speak in Gujarati!

JAGDEEP. Kiss my burning lips and calm me. Accept me also with a free mind. Say that I'm yours and I'll fling the roll of film outside the window.

SAVITA. No, no. Don't do that. I want to keep these photographs in special frames.

JAGDEEP *organizes the scene like a rape sequence in a Hindi film. He closes the door and sets the cassette player at a loud volume and in the din runs towards* SAVITA *to rape her. The song* Bachpan ke din bhula na dena *plays at ear-splitting levels.*

SAVITA (*screams*). You want to rape me? Definitely not. I will sacrifice this body but won't let you touch it.

SAVITA *moves to switch off the cassette player and* JAGDEEP *catches hold of her hand.*

JAGDEEP. Saali aurat! You've forgotten me! Who used to call out, Jaggu, Jaggu?

SAVITA. Jagdeep, leave me ... my hand ...

JAGDEEP. I love you from my heart!

SAVITA. What's the point in getting involved with somebody who doesn't have a shred of poetry in his blood? Get out! Savita is dead for you.

JAGDEEP. For me, you'll always be alive. This heart carries your image alone.

SAVITA. Jagdeep, what are you doing? You're using force on me! Rape!

JAGDEEP. Just one kiss! One!

SAVITA. A crumb of love thrown away in charity is useless!

JAGDEEP. Why are you stirring up a hornet's nest? The consequences will be very grim!

SAVITA. What'll you do? Rip apart this body? You want to kiss these ice-cold lips? What do you want to do?

JAGDEEP. I'll not tell you!

SAVITA. I've struck you off from my life.

JAGDEEP. Just once, call out my name just once!

SAVITA. I said No!

JAGDEEP. Let me kiss you once!

SAVITA. Never!

JAGDEEP. Just once, let me hold your hand with love!

SAVITA. Stay away. Get lost! I don't want your polluted hands to touch me!

RANCHOD *enters.*

SAVITA. You've returned early today?

RANCHOD. I had gone to collect dues from a customer. Waited there for half an hour. But his accountant didn't turn up.

SAVITA. That means you'll have to go early again tomorrow?

RANCHOD. I can't avoid that, can I? So, Jagdeep? Have you had tea?

SAVITA. I've been asking him for ages. He refuses.

RANCHOD. You can't go without having tea. Savita, Jagdeep is an affectionate man. How can we let him go empty handed?

JAGDEEP. Ranchoduncle, I'm getting late.

SAVITA. I made tea for Manilal, but Jagdeep's been in a big hurry ever since he arrived.

RANCHOD. You're fond of Manilal. But towards Jagdeep you have a mere sense of duty.

JAGDEEP. No, no. I really have to go.

RANCHOD. Yes, there is no way you can remain here. Hari, Hari. Your will prevails.

SAVITA. Jagdeep! Your camera!

JAGDEEP *leaves.* RANCHOD *sits on the cot. He reads* Jankalyan *and hums a bhajan.* SAVITA *gives* JAGDEEP *the camera and returns to chop vegetables.*

RANCHOD (*sings*). Let not your mind be affected by happiness or unhappiness/Born with this body you cannot avoid it/There is no king like Nala Raja, whose rani is Damyanti/He roamed the forests in tattered clothes, without food or water/The Five Pandavas, whose queen was Draupadi/Were banished to the forests for twelve years, their eyes were sleepless ...

SAVITA. Come and sit here.

RANCHOD. Let me complete the bhajan. (*Sings.*) There is no sati like Sita, whose lord was Rama/Ravana abducted her, and the sati was plunged in misery ... (RANCHOD *goes towards* SAVITA.) Why did you call me from Dinanath's?

SAVITA. Just like that.

RANCHOD. You have some work?

SAVITA. No, nothing.

RANCHOD. Then why did you call?

SAVITA. Talk to me. I'm lonely.

RANCHOD. I also feel lonely.

SAVITA. It'll be good to sit together for a few moments.

RANCHOD. Remember how we used to sit and talk to each other.

SAVITA. I say, is God omnipresent?

RANCHOD. He is.

SAVITA. Which means that He sees everything?

RANCHOD. Yes.

SAVITA. Even Sharmishtha and Navneet?

RANCHOD. Even Manilal.

SAVITA. Does He see us?

RANCHOD. Every moment.

SAVITA. But we can't see Him.

RANCHOD. I have.

SAVITA. Where is He?

RANCHOD. I can't see Him now.

SAVITA. You said you can see Him.

RANCHOD. I *have* seen Him once.

SAVITA. When?

RANCHOD. Remember, on our way back from our honeymoon we had gone to the seashore on a full moon night?

SAVITA. We were asleep on the terrace.

RANCHOD. That very night!

SAVITA. What?

RANCHOD. That night, Krishna sat on our cot and laughed.

SAVITA. What did you do?

RANCHOD. You think I'm shameless?

SAVITA. You're so shy. Worse than a woman.

RANCHOD. You need to have your clothes on in His presence.

SAVITA. That Krishna! That destroyer of homes is lodged in your mind. Since then this house hasn't been what it used to be.

RANCHOD. Why are you blaming Him?

SAVITA. Narsimha, Mira, Tukaram ... He destroyed their homes and He wasn't happy. Now, His evil eye has fallen on my house.

RANCHOD. Hari, Hari. Your will prevails.

Darkness.

SCENE 3

SHARMISHTHA's *house.* SHARMISHTHA *is cleaning the house as though she expects a special visitor. After sometime,* MANILAL *appears at the door.*

MANILAL. May I come in?

SHARMISHTHA. Who is it?

MANILAL. It's me, Manilal.

SHARMISHTHA. Come, come. Savita told me you'd be here in the afternoon.

MANILAL. Your house is nice and clean.

SHARMISHTHA. Don't poke fun at me.

MANILAL. Whatever I say you think I'm making fun of you.

SHARMISHTHA. I cleaned the house today.

MANILAL. Because I was going to visit you, isn't it? H'mmm, your sari is very expensive.

SHARMISHTHA. You like it, don't you? I like white.

MANILAL. It matches the colour of your body.

SHARMISHTHA. Should I make some tea?

MANILAL. No, I don't want tea.

SHARMISHTHA. Why?

MANILAL. I'll have milk.

SHARMISHTHA. Cold milk?

MANILAL. Something that will cool the heart.

SHARMISHTHA. Here, sit on the cot.

SHARMISHTHA *brings a glass of milk. In the meantime.* MANILAL *takes out a string of roses from his pocket.*

SHARMISHTHA. You've brought roses again.

MANILAL. See, how nice it looks with your sari.

SHARMISHTHA. Yes, but he doesn't like it.

MANILAL. What?

SHARMISHTHA. Roses.

MANILAL. Why? Does he have some kind of enmity towards flowers?

SHARMISHTHA. He asked me twice yesterday.

MANILAL. What?

SHARMISHTHA. Who gave you these flowers?

MANILAL. What did you say?

SHARMISHTHA. The truth.

MANILAL. What if he asks you today?

SHARMISHTHA. I'll tell him the truth. He never brings flowers. (*She gazes at* MANILAL *for a couple of seconds.*) Can I ask you something?

MANILAL. Why not?

SHARMISHTHA. Just because I ask you a question, you aren't to presume anything.

MANILAL. How can I presume before you ask the question?

SHARMISHTHA. You will tell Savita.

MANILAL. No, I won't.

SHARMISHTHA. Savita said that ...

MANILAL. What?

SHARMISHTHA. Savita said ...

MANILAL. What? What did she say?

SHARMISHTHA. Oh, forget it.

MANILAL. How can I let go now!

SHARMISHTHA. I feel shy to say it.

MANILAL. Look, I'll close my eyes. Then you can say what you want, right?

SHARMISHTHA. Savita said that you know how to woo with English poetry.

MANILAL. What about that?

SHARMISHTHA. What does it mean? I wonder how it feels to be wooed with English poetry?

MANILAL. Shall I demonstrate?

SHARMISHTHA. No, no. I just wanted to know.

MANILAL. How will you know without experiencing it?

SHARMISHTHA. Just tell me about it. She told me you sing too.

MANILAL. Doesn't Navneet do it?

SHARMISHTHA. He has no sense of rhythm. English poetry

is good, isn't it? Like the English themselves, fair and lovely.

MANILAL. And I?

SHARMISHTHA. You're an old man.

MANILAL. Look me in the eye and say it.

SHARMISHTHA. What?

MANILAL. That you don't like me.

SHARMISHTHA. There's nothing in your old face.

MANILAL. You've tied a hard stone round your heart.

SHARMISHTHA. I'm a sati savitri.

MANILAL. You want me to sing some poetry?

SHARMISHTHA. What if he comes to know?

MANILAL. How will he know?

SHARMISHTHA. What if Savita gets to know?

MANILAL. She will come to know! She doesn't have any objections.

SHARMISHTHA. Oh, I'll be so embarrassed!

MANILAL. Then don't tell her.

SHARMISHTHA. I'll have to.

MANILAL. Why?

SHARMISHTHA. She's like my elder sister.

MANILAL. Then come to me.

SHARMISHTHA. No.

MANILAL. Come, let's hold hands and dance.

Both dance. Darkness.

SCENE 4

SHARMISHTHA'*s house. She is engrossed in housework.* NAVNEET *enters wearing a kurta pyjama carrying a bag of books.* He flings his chappals to one side.

NAVNEET (*keeping the bag down*). I'm very tired today. Exhausted with tallying the accounts. I'll have to go early again tomorrow.

SHARMISHTHA. Do you want some tea?

NAVNEET. I've already had some. I got late so I had some snacks at the office.

SHARMISHTHA *gives him a glass of water.*

NAVNEET. What did you do all day?

SHARMISHTHA. The daily chores, what else? The flour had to be ground, the clothes had to be ironed. That's what I did. I was waiting for you. What shall I make for dinner?

NAVNEET. Bhakri and shaak! Where are you going?

SHARMISHTHA. I thought you have to meet Ranchodbhai.

NAVNEET. Sit here!

SHARMISHTHA. I should start cooking, shouldn't I?

NAVNEET (*looking at the wall*). Where's the photograph?

SHARMISHTHA. Which one?

NAVNEET. The one and only wedding photo we have.

SHARMISHTHA. I must have kept it somewhere while cleaning the house.

NAVNEET. You hardly give a damn, do you?

SHARMISHTHA. Did I say that?

NAVNEET. What do you mean you must have kept it somewhere? You don't even remember?

SHARMISHTHA. Of course I do. I've kept it in the cupboard.

NAVNEET. That means you didn't keep it away in a safe place while cleaning. You shoved it out of sight. Right?

SHARMISHTHA. I was scared.

NAVNEET. Of what?

SHARMISHTHA. That it would break as I cleaned and dusted the house.

NAVNEET. After all these years ... why did you have to be afraid today?

SHARMISHTHA. I'll get it from the cupboard and put it back.

SHARMISHTHA *goes towards the cupboard.* NAVNEET *sees the roses.*

NAVNEET. What's this forest doing in your hair?

SHARMISHTHA. Forest? What are you talking about?

NAVNEET. Look Sharmishtha, we can't afford to waste money on roses everyday.

SHARMISHTHA. I didn't buy them.

NAVNEET. Savita gave them to you?

SHARMISHTHA. No.

NAVNEET. Then who?

SHARMISHTHA. Manilal.

NAVNEET. Manilal? Who's that?

SHARMISHTHA. He knows Savita.

NAVNEET. You mean, this Manilal specially bought flowers for you?

SHARMISHTHA. No, no.

NAVNEET. Then?

SHARMISHTHA. He'd brought it for Savita. He had one extra. He gave me that.

NAVNEET. Gave it to you?

SHARMISHTHA. Yes ... no.

NAVNEET. Be clear, will you?

SHARMISHTHA. You're suspicious about the smallest of things. Why?

NAVNEET. I go away to the office in the morning and return only in the evening. You're alone at home all day ...

SHARMISHTHA. There's Savita.

NAVNEET (*dismissively*). Yes, but ... one can never be too sure of her, can one?

SHARMISHTHA. Why do you say that?

NAVNEET. Savita is different. And so's her acquaintance. What did you say his name was?

SHARMISHTHA. Manilal! Manilal!

NAVNEET. You take his name as though you're inhaling the fragrance of those roses!

SHARMISHTHA. I told you because you asked.

NAVNEET. Yes, but there's a difference in the way you utter his name.

SHARMISHTHA. You'll quarrel even with the wind.

NAVNEET. I don't want any more roses in the house after today, all right.

SHARMISHTHA. Why don't you ever get me anything?

NAVNEET. What? What have I not got for you?

SHARMISHTHA. What have you ever got for me?

NAVNEET. What do you want?

SHARMISHTHA. *You* have to think about that.

NAVNEET. What do we need, we have everything. (*Suddenly his eyes fall on her sari.*) You've worn a new sari at home!

SHARMISHTHA. Looks good, doesn't it?

NAVNEET. So? Do you have to wear a new sari at home?

SHARMISHTHA. I like to wear different saris at home. Don't you like fresh meals everyday?

NAVNEET. If you like new things so much, why don't you throw me away? Or pawn me off to the vasanwala like an old shirt! That should satisfy you.

SHARMISHTHA (*muttering*). No vasanwala would give even two tablespoons in exchange for you.

NAVNEET (*shouting*). What did you say?

SHARMISHTHA *quickly goes out.* NAVNEET *is left staring.*

Darkness.

SCENE 5

SAVITA's *house.* RANCHOD *is reading the* Jankalyan *aloud.* NAVNEET *enters.*

RANCHOD. How do you save yourself from the dangers of Kaliyug? Concentrate on God. Immerse yourself in Him. Just once. And see the miracle. Vishnu will appear before you on the Pushpak Viman. He will say to Lakshmi sitting at his feet. Let it be, let it be. My devotees are desperate.

NAVNEET. Ranchod! Ranchod!

RANCHOD. Prabhu will seat you in the Viman and knock at the doors of Swarg. The grandeur of Swarg will be revealed. The dance of the apsaras, the song of the kinnaras, royal swans feeding on pearls ...

NAVNEET. Where's Sharmishtha?

RANCHOD. She and Savita have suddenly become very interested in cooking. Both have gone to buy recipe books.

NAVNEET. Do you understand what that means?

RANCHOD (*closing the* Jankalyan *and keeping it aside*). Lady Luck is smiling on us.

NAVNEET. What do you mean?

RANCHOD. We'll get to eat new dishes everyday.

NAVNEET (*strikes his forehead*). This is the limit!

RANCHOD. What's troubling you?

NAVNEET. Don't pretend.

RANCHOD. What about?

NAVNEET. Can't you see? He gives them roses everyday.

RANCHOD. Who wears them?

NAVNEET. Sharmishtha.

RANCHOD. So what? Savita wears mogras everyday.

NAVNEET. She sings in the evening.

RANCHOD. Is there a ban on singing?

NAVNEET. She bought a white sari and wore it the same day!

RANCHOD. Savita has two white saris.

NAVNEET. She says white saris match very well with roses.

RANCHOD. I'll never understand women.

NAVNEET. Do you know what's been going on behind your back?

RANCHOD. I don't even know what is going on in front of my eyes. How will I know what's going on behind my back?

NAVNEET. You're pathetic and unworldly, aren't you?

RANCHOD. What have you gained by being worldly?

NAVNEET. I'm enraged at what's going on behind our backs.

RANCHOD. Now you seem to be claiming your rights as a husband.

NAVNEET. Don't you want to put an end to all this?

RANCHOD. I'm a lover of the spirit. I've long since lost all desires of the flesh. I am more concerned about the soul.

NAVNEET. You're not affected at all?

RANCHOD. To feel or not to feel. Mere illusion.

NAVNEET. Manilal should be beaten up and stuffed with chillies.

RANCHOD. Look Navneet, when our loved ones love another human being we should be happy.

NAVNEET. Manilal should be killed right here, in the chawl itself.

RANCHOD. You will not get Sharmishtha by doing that. You'll lose her forever.

NAVNEET. Oh Ranchod! What should I do?

RANCHOD. You should celebrate Sharmishtha's love.

NAVNEET. Never. I'll kill him. Drink his blood.

RANCHOD. You will wash the sins of your last birth.

NAVNEET. That's not possible in this birth.

RANCHOD. Don't say such things. You remind me of Jagdeep.

NAVNEET. Why Jagdeep?

RANCHOD. He's also frightened. Like you.

NAVNEET. What do you mean Like me?

RANCHOD. You are both helpless.

NAVNEET. Helpless?

RANCHOD. Jagdeep was begging Savita.

NAVNEET. That rascal Mania must be laughing at us! We should make mincemeat of him.

RANCHOD. What difference will that make?

NAVNEET. Come with me! Right Now!

RANCHOD. Where?

NAVNEET. To Jagdeep.

RANCHOD. Why?

NAVNEET. I need his help to confront Mania.

RANCHOD. I don't have any problems with Manilal.

NAVNEET. But I do!

RANCHOD. Then you go.

NAVNEET. Are you on my side or Manilal's?

RANCHOD. I belong to no party. But ... if you say so I'll go with you.

NAVNEET *and* RANCHOD *leave.*

Darkness.

SCENE 6

JAGDEEP's *house.* JAGDEEP *hangs a noose around his neck and looks at* SAVITA's *photograph on the string.*

JAGDEEP (*in Hindi*). Kyon mere dil ko patthar se takraya? Kyon mujhe kya se kya banaya? Why did this happen? Why didn't that happen? Because I don't have a mother? I want to give up my life. Because my mother is dead. Life has suddenly become desolate. Why? Because I don't have a mother. Oh, Ma! I am coming, to you, Ma! This two-timing woman has hurled me away. She has wrecked me. Is this why she loved me? Oh, how I used to lift her tresses! Ma, today you are not here and I miss you so much. (NAVNEET *and* RANCHOD *can be seen outside the house.* NAVNEET *knocks on the door.*) Who is it? Go away! This beautiful woman has rejected me. I will reject the world. (NAVNEET *knocks on the door again.*) I await Death. This door will not open for anybody else! Go away!

NAVNEET (*disguises his voice*). Postman! Postman!

JAGDEEP. Postman? At this time?

NAVNEET (*in the same voice*). Money order! Money order!

JAGDEEP *opens the door.*

JAGDEEP. Ranchoduncle?

NAVNEET. Let us in.

JAGDEEP. Why?

NAVNEET. These things can't be discussed on the doorstep.

JAGDEEP. Wait, let me organize the room. (*He closes the door, upturns* SAVITA's *photograph on the table and opens the door.* RANCHOD *and* NAVNEET *enter.*) Ranchoduncle, why did my mother die?

RANCHOD. Fate. It's not your fault.

JAGDEEP. Had she been alive she would've saved me today!

NAVNEET. Have faith. Aren't I here?

JAGDEEP. People worship false love like gold. I'm sick of this uncaring world.

NAVNEET. You'll not help me?

JAGDEEP. Why do you need help?

NAVNEET. For the same reason that you are sick of this uncaring world.

JAGDEEP. I don't understand.

NAVNEET. How do I start?

JAGDEEP. You don't want to? Then let it be.

NAVNEET. No, no. I'll tell you. My wife wears her best saris at home and has roses in her hair. She hums all day. And now she's cooking new dishes everyday.

JAGDEEP. You don't know how to woo with English nursery rhymes, do you?

NAVNEET. No.

JAGDEEP. And you, Ranchoduncle?

RANCHOD. I love the soul.

JAGDEEP. I want to kill myself.

NAVNEET. Why?

JAGDEEP. Because I don't know English nursery rhymes. And my mother is dead.

RANCHOD. Her time had come. Yours has not.

NAVNEET. You'll not support me?

JAGDEEP. Who supported me! I held her hand. And she? She showed me the door.

RANCHOD. To love the body ... that is only skindeep.

NAVNEET. Revenge! Take revenge, Jagdeep! Dig your nails into him and skin him, saala.

RANCHOD. Navneet!

NAVNEET. You've suffered so much. You are heartbroken. Your love is splintered into a thousand pieces. Let him go through the same thing.

RANCHOD. Navneet! Are you insane?

NAVNEET. Yes, I've gone mad. I want to grind his body into itsy-bitsy pieces and feed it to rabid dogs.

RANCHOD. Keep your cool, Navneet! Please.

JAGDEEP. Had my mother been alive, none of this would've happened.

NAVNEET. Saala, whip him!

JAGDEEP. Ma, had I ever done anything to that Manilal? Don't embarrass me, Uncle. I'm standing at death's door. Forgive me.

RANCHOD. What had to happen has happened. You are not to blame. It is your fate.

JAGDEEP. You're truly great, Uncle. And I? I wanted to blackmail your Savita! I wanted to frighten her and get back her love! I blackmailed her, and she dismissed my threats with a wave of her hands. I wanted to show you these photographs.

RANCHOD *picks up the heap of photographs on the table and looks through them.* JAGDEEP *is confused at this.* RANCHOD *shows* NAVNEET *a photograph.*

RANCHOD. See, Navneet! I always knew Savita was photogenic. See how her laughter blossoms.

NAVNEET. Doesn't this affect you?

RANCHOD. Why? I'm happy.

NAVNEET. No jealousy?

JAGDEEP. It was here that she brought spring into my autumnal life. In your absence I made merry with Savita here. Right here, her touch has aroused my desire. I dropped four catches in the match and our team lost ... and now this room has become the land of my death.

RANCHOD. Everything else will go according to the wheels of fate. But you shouldn't have dropped those catches. That was wrong.

NAVNEET. You'd go to the office, come home and read *Jankalyan* and do your prayers. While he would make merry here with your wife. That's not wrong. But he was wrong to drop catches?

RANCHOD. Yes. We had to accept defeat against the neighbours.

NAVNEET. Enough! I can't bear it anymore. (*He leaves the room.*)

RANCHOD. Jagdeep, when the person we love falls in love with another, it should make us happy.

JAGDEEP. It's too late. Spring has turned to autumn.

RANCHOD. You were attached to the body. Hungry passion will never allow you to see pure love.

JAGDEEP. Don't utter a single word, Ranchoduncle! Life is now a complete zero.

RANCHOD. I'm telling you the truth. It's not worthwhile throwing away your life for Savita. You take good photographs. Why don't you take up photography?

Darkness.

SCENE 7

SHARMISHTHA's *house.* SHARMISHTHA *and* SAVITA *are poring over the recipe book.*

SHARMISHTHA. There are all kinds of shaak and farsaan in here, some that we haven't even heard of.

SAVITA. It says Tasty, nutritious old and new vegetarian snacks.

SHARMISHTHA. What does Vegetarian mean?

SAVITA. Recipe book, that's what it means. But what are you going to make?

SHARMISHTHA. Green pea patties.

SAVITA. You'll impress everybody.

SHARMISHTHA. My head is swimming.

SAVITA. Why?

SHARMISHTHA. It's very difficult.

SAVITA. What?

SHARMISHTHA. Boil 625 grammes of peas in 200 grammes of water, take 25 grammes butter.

SAVITA. What's wrong with that?

SHARMISHTHA. Cook with a weighing scale?

SAVITA. Love demands the ultimate sacrifice.

SHARMISHTHA. Did I deny that? But the shaakwala doesn't give 625 grammes of peas. He grins when I ask for two grammes chillies and three inches of ginger.

SAVITA. That's true.

SHARMISHTHA. I take two handfuls of daal and rice, add three pinches of turmeric and five pinches of salt and khichdi is ready. This book says Sosh. What's that?

SAVITA. Not Sosh, Sauce.

SHARMISHTHA. Sosh.

SAVITA. Sauce.

SHARMISHTHA. What's Sauce?

SAVITA. A masala you add in soup.

SHARMISHTHA. Soup?

SAVITA. Soup.

SHARMISHTHA. What's that?

SAVITA. The water in which you boil daal.

SHARMISHTHA. What are you going to make?

SAVITA. The first item, tomato jalebi.

SHARMISHTHA. Are you crazy?

SAVITA. It says so in the book.

SHARMISHTHA. What?

SAVITA. Your guests will end up licking their fingers.

SHARMISHTHA. What nonsense?

SAVITA. It's not easy to make. Tomatoes have to be peeled first.

SHARMISHTHA. What? How?

SAVITA. With a pair of small tongs, the kind a watch repairer has.

SHARMISHTHA. Is it written in here?

SAVITA. Yes. It says here one tomato will take half an hour to peel!

SHARMISHTHA. How many jalebis will we need?

SAVITA. Your bhai, Navneetbhai, you, me, The four of us ... and Manilal likes jalebies. And then I'm going to make them. That means, twenty jalebies, how many hours would that take?

SHARMISHTHA. Twenty jalebies would mean at least ten hours.

SAVITA. Time ... It has no meaning when it comes to love.

SHARMISHTHA. Then, what do you do after that?

SAVITA. Dip the peeled tomatoes in sugar syrup.

SHARMISHTHA. I've never seen a naked tomato.

SAVITA. I'll see naked tomatoes. I'll call you if you want to.

SHARMISHTHA. What do you fry them in?

SAVITA. It says Deep fry them.

SHARMISHTHA. What is Deep fry?

SAVITA. Steam cook in hot ghee.

SHARMISHTHA. Did Jagdeep come to meet you afterwards?

SAVITA. He had come to pollute this body, each cell of which has been purified by Manilal's touch. He turned on the radio loud declaring that he would rape me! He begged me for a kiss, he wanted an embrace. That Jagdeep had come to knock at the doors of my heart. If his fingers had as much as touched me, how could I have taken a corrupt body to Kashmir with Manilal?

SHARMISHTHA. Ever since Manilal said Tell everybody if you want to come to Kashmir, my head has been swimming.

SAVITA. Why? It's because the Kashmir visit can be a problem that we're taking such pains, aren't we? Tomato jalebi, pumpkin subji and onion daal.

SHARMISHTHA. He'll not be fooled like Ranchodbhai. I'm telling you, he won't come for the party.

SAVITA. Don't worry.

SHARMISHTHA. I see myself in hospital for six months. He'll beat me. It's nothing new for him.

SAVITA. I'll talk to your bhai. He'll explain it to him.

SHARMISHTHA. After I talk to him about Kashmir it'll be like taking a dip in the Ganga and crossing the Gomti.

Darkness.

SCENE 8

NAVNEET *tries to go through the passage.* SAVITA *stops him.*

NAVNEET. Will you step aside?

SAVITA. Which side?

NAVNEET. Any side!

SAVITA. Why?

NAVNEET. I want to go.

SAVITA. Why, what has happened?

NAVNEET. I'm very tired. I want to go home and have Sharmishtha make me a cup of tea.

SAVITA. I have some work with you.

NAVNEET. Later.

SAVITA. I want to tell you something.

NAVNEET. I don't have the time. What is it that you want to tell me?

SAVITA. Tonight, at my place ...

NAVNEET. What's happening at your place? Be quick!

SAVITA. You make me speak at the point of a gun!

NAVNEET. If you don't want to tell me, let it be.

SAVITA. You don't want to hear?

NAVNEET. What is it that you want to say?

SAVITA. You have to come to my place for dinner. You and Sharmishtha ...

NAVNEET. We'll come. Why did you waste so much time for that? (SAVITA *lets* NAVNEET *pass.* NAVNEET *goes, then suddenly turns around.*) Just a minute, is Mania going to be there?

SAVITA. Mania?

NAVNEET. Your Manilal.

SAVITA. My Manilal?

NAVNEET. Don't pretend.

SAVITA. But Manilal is not mine. He belongs to everybody.

NAVNEET. Whatever. Is he coming?

SAVITA. Yes. And Sharmishtha's been helping me with the food at my place for some time.

NAVNEET. I'm not coming. And send Sharmishtha home. I want to have some tea.

SAVITA. Have it at my place.

NAVNEET. No.

RANCHOD *enters the chawl.*

NAVNEET. Ranchod, you tell her. I can't be like you.

RANCHOD. What's up?

SAVITA. I invited him home for dinner and he got mad.

NAVNEET. I don't want to be near that devil's shadow. He should be shot dead.

RANCHOD. Who do you want to shoot today?

NAVNEET. Mania.

RANCHOD. Enough, you don't need to say anymore. (*To* SAVITA.) You go home and prepare the food. I'll bring him.

NAVNEET. Didn't I say No!

Darkness.

SCENE 9

SHARMISHTHA's *house.* RANCHOD *and* NAVNEET *enter.*

RANCHOD. You're getting needlessly provoked.

NAVNEET. *I* am getting needlessly provoked?

RANCHOD. Yes, you're foolish. Think a bit. Onion daal and pumpkin shaak, pea patties and tomato jalebies. Give up all this for Manilal?

NAVNEET (*surprised*). Tomato jalebi?

RANCHOD. I'm thinking of calling Jagdeep too.

NAVNEET. He is a naive fool.

RANCHOD. He's naive, but he's not a loafer.

NAVNEET. You're an ass. Tomato jalebi? Impossible. The whole business stinks.

RANCHOD. I've seen colourful pictures in the recipe book.

NAVNEET. Tomato jalebi! For that cunning good-for-nothing who roams around with a dozen strings of flowers in his pocket!

RANCHOD. He probably likes flowers.

NAVNEET. Hahn bhai, Hahn. He probably has a garden of flowers. He may own the Vrindavan Gardens for all I care. I don't want to share anything with him.

RANCHOD. Round, red tomatoes glistening with syrup.

NAVNEET. What?

RANCHOD. Pictures of tomato jalebies

NAVNEET. What size are they?

RANCHOD (*spreads his fingers and shows*). This big.

NAVNEET. But they're not making it for us.

RANCHOD. If they were only meant for Manilal why would they tell us?

NAVNEET. I feel tempted, but ...

RANCHOD. What are you waiting for then?

NAVNEET. I won't be able to control myself if that Mania is there.

RANCHOD. Don't speak a word. Eat it all up quietly.

NAVNEET. Are we some kind of thieves to eat quietly? You go home. Send Sharmishtha, I want to have some tea. No, no. I'm not going to come. Day before yesterday, as I was coming back home from the bank I saw Mania in a taxi with a woman. I recognized him immediately. He was not paying attention. When I meet him I'm going to tell him, You, Mania, you are a cunning rascal, you're a luccha, lafanga, dhoorth.

RANCHOD. That's your opinion. It is possible that it may change tomorrow.

NAVNEET. My opinion of Mania? Not at all! Never.

RANCHOD. Navneet, only God is constant. Opinions, love and desire are like chameleons. They change colour with each passing moment.

NAVNEET. My opinion of Mania will never change.

RANCHOD. After marriage I desired Savita passionately. Morning and noon my vision was filled with her. I would come home from the office and my heart would overflow with love. Then Jagdeep started coming home. I would burn with jealousy. Love disappeared like the colours of a butterfly's wings. My faith in God deepened. Now, I pity Jagdeep.

NAVNEET. Then what *is* the Truth?

RANCHOD (*takes* NAVNEET *to the window*). See the leaves of that tree illuminated by the streetlight. The leaves look blue at night. In the morning the light of the sun makes them look yellow. We say that leaves are green. What is the truth? I have seen all the colours of the chameleon. Come, wash yourself. They must me waiting for us.

NAVNEET. No, I won't come.

RANCHOD. Don't bury your head in the sand like an ostrich.

NAVNEET. Your statements should be framed and kept in every house. This is society, and society has some rules. Words don't work in society, rules do.

RANCHOD. Why should there be a difference between the truth and social norms?

NAVNEET. Because there is a difference.

Silence.

RANCHOD. Whose side are you in? Mine or Manilal's?

NAVNEET. Yours.

RANCHOD. Then come. Wash yourself. Jagdeep must be waiting for us.

Darkness.

SCENE 10

RANCHOD's *house.* SAVITA *and* SHARMISHTHA *are in white nylon saris preparing to welcome the guests.*

SAVITA. The jalebies can't be soggy.

SHARMISHTHA. Finally they hardened, didn't they. Baap, those tomato jalebies took the life out of us!

SAVITA. Manilal likes strong and firm things, doesn't he?

SHARMISHTHA. Yes, he said so. What is that you are pasting on your lips?

SAVITA. Lipstick.

SHARMISHTHA. No, we can't colour our lips!

SAVITA. Manilal gave it to me.

SHARMISHTHA. Show it to me, what's it called?

SAVITA. Lipstick.

SHARMISHTHA. Lipstick! Can I use it too?

SAVITA. Come let me put it for you.

SHARMISHTHA. I don't even have a matching blouse.

SAVITA. This is nice.

SHARMISHTHA. Oh! My lips feel sticky.

SAVITA. Now you'll be able to speak in English.

SHARMISHTHA. How come?

SAVITA. Because the English apply lipstick twice a day.

SHARMISHTHA. I'm very scared.

SAVITA. Why be afraid of telling the truth? Doesn't Manilal say that Truth is indestructible?

SHARMISHTHA. Ever since Manilal said that if you want to go to Kashmir, tell everybody, my head's been whirling.

SAVITA. He won't avoid your bhai. I'm confident of that.

SHARMISHTHA. Your bhai will fly off his temper if he sees Manilal here. I can see myself in hospital for six months.

SAVITA. Shall we wear our saris the Bengali way today?

SHARMISHTHA. What for?

SAVITA. For moral strength.

Darkness.

SCENE 11

SAVITA's *house.* SAVITA *and* SHARMISHTHA *are ready and are waiting impatiently. Suddenly ...*

SAVITA-SHARMISHTHA. What's the time?

Both burst into laughter. SAVITA *peeps out of the window.*

SAVITA. He's here! Are you ready?

SHARMISHTHA. I've been ready a long time.

MANILAL *enters.*

SAVITA. One ... two ... three!

SHARMISHTHA (*chanting*) My string of roses ... Maujila Manilal!

SAVITA (*chanting*). The owner of my mogra string ... Maujila Manilal!

SHARMISHTHA. The quencher of the thirst of yugs.

SAVITA. The vagabond of the Kashmir valley.

SHARMISHTHA. The scaler of Pahalgaon's hills.

SAVITA-SHARMISHTHA. Maujila Manilal! Maujila Manilal!

SAVITA. My source of inspiration, he'll love me in the mountains.

SHARMISHTHA. He, who has spilt the wine of my youth, will imprison me in the forests of Jhelum.

All three of them hold hands and dance.

MANILAL. Baa baa, black sheep/Have you any wool/Yes sir, yes sir/Three bags full/One for my master/One for my dame/ One for the little girl/Who lives down the lane.

The three of them stand still. RANCHOD *enters with* NAVNEET *and* JAGDEEP.

NAVNEET (*sarcastically*). The house gleams.

RANCHOD. It is like Diwali.

NAVNEET. Oh, there's rangoli too!

MANILAL. How are you?

RANCHOD (*to* MANILAL). Welcome.

JAGDEEP. Ranchoduncle, can I leave?

RANCHOD. No, no. You specially have to be here.

JAGDEEP (*in Hindi*). Mujhe use ek bar dekhna hai.

NAVNEET (*to* JAGDEEP). I'll hit you, if you speak in Hindi once more.

RANCHOD (*to* SAVITA). I have brought Jagdeep along.

SAVITA (*crossly, to* RANCHOD). You always mess up things. Why the hell did you bring him here?

MANILAL. You are Navneetlal?

NAVNEET. Yes, why?

MANILAL. Are you interested in the share market?

NAVNEET. Yes, why?

MANILAL. What do you think of the recent troubles in the market?

In a huff, NAVNEET *sits at a distance from* MANILAL. MANILAL *asks* SAVITA *for some water.*

SAVITA (*whispers*). Sharmishtha, give Manilal some water.

SHARMISHTHA (*whispers*). No, no. You give it.

SAVITA. Be strong and give it, he won't say anything in front of everybody.

SHARMISHTHA (*whispers*). I see myself in hospital for six months.

SAVITA (*whispers*). You want to go to Kashmir, don't you?

SHARMISHTHA *gives* MANILAL *a glass of water.* SHARMISHTHA *and* NAVNEET *are face-to-face.*

JAGDEEP (*glaring at* MANILAL, *he chants*). Jaane woh kaise log the jinko do do pyar mila ...

NAVNEET. Quiet! I told you not to speak in Hindi! Get out!

SAVITA (*to* RANCHOD). Why did you bring him along? As though he's the life of the party!

JAGDEEP. Ranchoduncle, why did you insist on my coming?

NAVNEET (*to* RANCHOD). You should've let him die. Why did you save him?

JAGDEEP. Ma, main aa raha hoon ... May I leave Ranchoduncle?

SAVITA (*to* JAGDEEP). Why do you keep asking? Go if you want to!

MANILAL (*to* JAGDEEP). You didn't bring our photographs?

NAVNEET (*to* MANILAL). Yesterday, Jagdeep was about to kill himself. I saved him.

MANILAL (*to* NAVNEET). Congratulations!

RANCHOD. Can we discuss this after dinner?

NAVNEET. No. Jagdeep, you'll have to answer me in front of everybody. Who drove you to tie a noose round your neck? Ranchod, Savita or Manilal?

RANCHOD. His fate.

NAVNEET (*to* RANCHOD). Who asked you? (*To* JAGDEEP.) Who do you think is responsible?

JAGDEEP. My mother.

NAVNEET. How?

JAGDEEP. She died.

NAVNEET. This Mania destroyed your life, didn't he?

MANILAL (*to* NAVNEET). The name is Manilal.

NAVNEET. This, this one ... he's the one who destroyed you.

JAGDEEP. How?

NAVNEET. He snatched Savita from you.

JAGDEEP. Had my mother been alive, nobody would've dared to steal Savita from me.

SAVITA. That means you weren't giving up your life for me?

JAGDEEP. No.

SAVITA. Then why did you come here?

JAGDEEP. Ranchoduncle insisted that I come for dinner. So I thought I could take one last look at you. Savita, you look very beautiful.

RANCHOD. Navneet, didn't I tell you?

NAVNEET. What?

RANCHOD. That Savita looks beautiful. And now Jagdeep has declared it in public.

MANILAL. Whatever the reason Jagdeepbhai, why did you decide to kill yourself?

JAGDEEP. Suicide is preferable to murder.

MANILAL. Why?

JAGDEEP. If you don't see it, you don't get burnt.

NAVNEET. That means that you didn't want to end your life only because of your mother, right?

JAGDEEP. Yes.

NAVNEET. What was the other reason?

JAGDEEP. They threw me out of the cricket team too. Had Ma been alive, I would've lived through it.

NAVNEET. He's a complete coward!

MANILAL (*to* JAGDEEP). Why? It isn't Savita, is it?

JAGDEEP. She slammed the door of love on my face. She used to call me Jaggu but now she refuses to.

MANILAL. Is it all right if I call you Jaggu instead?

JAGDEEP. No!

SAVITA. I have thrown him out of my life.

JAGDEEP. Call me Jaggu once!

SAVITA. I said No!

JAGDEEP. Once!

SAVITA. No, no, no!

JAGDEEP. Tumne mera dil tod diya! I'm leaving. I'll never return!

SAVITA. Keep your word.

MANILAL. Savita! Don't be so harsh. The poor thing is pleading. Just call him Jaggu once. What does it matter?

SAVITA. If you say so. Jaggu! Enough?

JAGDEEP. Yeh tumhara akhri tohfa bhi kubool. Now I shall go and ask the night to stop. Ranchoduncle, no. Don't stop me.

MANILAL (*pointing towards* JAGDEEP, *sings*). Gujare je shira ...

JAGDEEP *goes out.*

RANCHOD. Jagdeep!

RANCHOD *follows him.*

NAVNEET. Ranchod! Ranchod! He will lapse into Hindi again.

NAVNEET *follows* RANCHOD.

SAVITA (*whispers*). Now, you be strong and tell him.

SHARMISHTHA (*whispers*). You saw his reaction, didn't you? He walks around with a ton of anger in his pockets.

NAVNEET *returns, stands near the window and listens to their conversation which is going on in whispers.*

SAVITA. You will have to tell him!

SHARMISHTHA. You tell him!

SAVITA. Tell whom?

SHARMISHTHA. Ranchodbhai, when he's there.

SAVITA. What should I say?

SHARMISHTHA. That we're going to Kashmir.

SAVITA. Be clear.

SHARMISHTHA. Why?

SAVITA. Because he'll immediately have questions. We'll have to tell him everything.

SHARMISHTHA. Then do it.

SAVITA. What?

SHARMISHTHA (*louder*). Tell him that Sharmishtha and I are going to Kashmir with Manilal in a white Ambassador car.

NAVNEET *enters.*

NAVNEET. What did you say? What was that again?

SAVITA. She was saying ...

NAVNEET. For God's sake, will you let her speak?

SHARMISHTHA. Savita and I are going to Kashmir.

NAVNEET. You and Savita, alone?

SAVITA. No, we ...

NAVNEET. Did I ask you? Why do you keep interfering? Tell me, who are you going with?

SHARMISHTHA. Manilal.

NAVNEET. Why?

SHARMISHTHA. He's going to get a new white Ambassador car.

NAVNEET. Is everybody who is getting a new white Ambassador going to Kashmir this season? And do you have to go with each one of them?

SHARMISHTHA (*imitates* MANILAL, *with a flair*). If possible!

NAVNEET. Ranchod! Ranchod!

SHARMISHTHA. We are going only for one and a half months. Why are you shouting?

NAVNEET. So you'll burn the house down and then proceed on a pilgrimage?

SHARMISHTHA. We're going for a trip! We are not burning the house down.

NAVNEET. Ranchod!

RANCHOD *enters.*

RANCHOD. What is it?

NAVNEET. Sharmishtha, Savita and ... this, this ...

MANILAL. Manilal.

NAVNEET. The three want to go to Kashmir for a trip!

MANILAL. We're planning to leave on the twentieth.

SAVITA. Manilal is going to get a brand new fairy of a white Ambassador car. Two days in Udaipur, one day in Delhi and then Srinagar. We will rent a houseboat on Dal Lake.

MANILAL. Ah, to stay in a houseboat. The ultimate fulfilment for lovers.

RANCHOD. I've heard that it gets pretty cold at this time of the year. Savita, keep your shawl with you.

SHARMISHTHA. Learn, learn from your friend. (NAVNEET *slaps* SHARMISHTHA.) Didn't I tell you? I'm not surprised that he hit me. (*Cries.*)

SAVITA. Showing your virility?

RANCHOD. Navneet, I am ashamed of you today.

MANILAL. It is not right to lift your hand on a sensible, cultured, arya woman.

SAVITA. You hit my frightened friend. Your hands will sprout thorns.

MANILAL. Foul language! From you?

SHARMISHTHA. I'll bear such pain. But I will go, will go and will go to Kashmir.

NAVNEET. I'll file a police complaint.

SAVITA. May you fall in the roaring depths of hell.

MANILAL. What chaste language! See the miracles that flow from it.

NAVNEET. Sharmishtha, I'm telling you for the last time. You'll go to Kashmir over my dead body.

RANCHOD. Navneet, how can you stake such a claim on her?

NAVNEET. Ranchod, what's going on? Have I not done anything for her!

MANILAL. What havc you donc? Whcn have you got roses for Sharmishtha? Ranchodbhai, who got mogras for Savita? You haven't even given Savita a proper look. Never bought saris for her. Navneet doesn't want to buy a chiffon sari for Sharmishtha. How innocent Sharmishtha looks in two plaits! But Navneet doesn't know it. When Sharmishtha wears roses, she sports matching chappals. And Navneet? Has he ever noticed? No! What injustice! You married a woman and brought her home. That's all. You kept her in a corner like a Storewell cupboard, trapped her in the four walls of the kitchen and chained her to the bed. Then you jump on her and have sex. Tell me, do you know who sits up all night and makes the dough for papad? Who makes the chutney? Who garnishes the daal with coriander? Who puts elaichi skin in tea made from pure milk? Who buys basmati rice and puts ghee on hot chapattis?

Everybody is stunned.

JAGDEEP *enters the room. He has a noose round his neck and is preparing to die.*

JAGDEEP. Hé Vishwaniyanta! You snatched my mother from me. Tujhe dukh nahin hua. Savita considered me her own and showered her love on me. She is not mine anymore. How I used to score boundaries in cricket, I have even scored a century ... And now? Pain ... pain ... pain does not leave me. Impossible to live. Death is the only answer. Ma! Why did you give birth to me? Main aa raha hoon tere paas. (*Chants.*) O, orphaned child ...

JAGDEEP *dies.*

Darkness.

Interval

ACT II

SCENE 1

Darkness.

RANCHOD'S *voice, in a monotonous chant.* Satyug was the era of Ramrajya. In that yug, there was no need to have sexual relations to conceive. Chant a mantra, call the Gods, and women would conceive. Then came Dwaparyug. Chant a mantra, and words would disperse in the air. A mere touch was enough for conception. In Tretayug a kiss was all you needed. The rishis gave Kumari Kunti a mantra in the Mahabharata. Kunti, in a playful mood, tried the mantra out on Surya Dev. As soon as she did that, light flooded the earth! In a split second Kunti was unconscious. Raja Mahendra of the Ikshwaku dynasty had no heirs. The raja suffered from many illnesses. Then Indra Dev took the form of Mahendra and entered Queen Rambha's quarters. He indulged in rati-kreeda with her. The Ikshwaku dynasty continued. Kaliyug! Kaliyug brought physical relations with it. Princes were instructed by courtesans. They learned the latest sexual knowhow from the ganikas whose status in society declined. They forgot the essence of Vatsyayana's teachings. They forgot the essence of love, the goodness of it. Love was swept aside. There was a curtain on the eyes of knowledge. Let us remove the curtains, let us get ready to banish darkness. Let us create Ramrajya once more.

SCENE 2

SHARMISHTHA's *house. Afternoon.* SAVITA *and* SHARMISHTHA *are sitting on the cot, engrossed in conversation.*

SHARMISHTHA. Read the letter!

SAVITA. It's personal.

SHARMISHTHA. Who delivered it?

SAVITA. The postman.

SHARMISHTHA. Read it!

SAVITA. On one condition.

SHARMISHTHA. What?

SAVITA. You repeat what I say.

SHARMISHTHA. All right.

SAVITA. Repeat. A hundred salutes to Jagdeep who wrote one last letter of farewell and then sacrificed himself for love.

SHARMISHTHA. I salute him. Now read the letter!

SAVITA (*reads*). My dear life Savita, you rejected me because I could not recite nursery rhymes. Tune theek kiya. English should be our mother tongue. It would be so pleasant if all Gujaratis could speak English. But our politicians do not understand this. I studied in Vasad. There was no trace of English there. By the time I came to Mumbai it was too late. It is my failing that I cannot recite nursery rhymes in English. I cannot live without you. That is why I will sacrifice my life and prove my love. Your crazy lover, Jagdeep ... He writes so well, doesn't he? And I thought he was only a good photographer.

SHARMISHTHA. You were right!

SAVITA. About?

SHARMISHTHA. His love turned out to be as true as our love. What do you think? If I write a suicide note and kill myself, will Manilal recite nursery rhymes for me for all time to come?

SAVITA. Manilal's a social animal. He isn't interested in the dead.

Darkness.

SCENE 3

Hell. JAGDEEP *regains consciousness.*

JAGDEEP. Where am I?

YAMRAJ *enters. He wears the traditional dress seen in the calendars.*

YAMRAJ. You! Chokro, what did you do?

JAGDEEP. Who are you?

YAMRAJ. Who do I look like?

JAGDEEP. A gurkha.

YAMRAJ. Listen, chokro, I am Yamraj himself.

JAGDEEP. Why? What did I do?

YAMRAJ. Suicide.

JAGDEEP. A sacrifice for love!

YAMRAJ. Ill-timed sacrifice is like white silk. It reveals as much as it hides.

JAGDEEP. I don't understand.

YAMRAJ. You say that you sacrificed your life. Who asked for it, and who accepted it? Chokro, your time was not up. You rushed into it impatiently and landed here.

JAGDEEP. That means, I'm not needed here too?

YAMRAJ. You were needed on the earth. You were fated to marry Shankarbhai's daughter, Rekha.

JAGDEEP. But she ran away with Lalu.

YAMRAJ. You confused man! She was going to return in a week's time. Who asked you to get into this mess with Savita?

JAGDEEP. She didn't value my love.

YAMRAJ. You were running after Savita like cattle without a master. That was your love, wasn't it!

JAGDEEP. It was impossible to live without Savita.

YAMRAJ. Don't lie. You wanted to teach her a lesson.

JAGDEEP. What?

YAMRAJ. You wanted her pity.

JAGDEEP. I wanted her love.

YAMRAJ. You did not get love, so you committed suicide, you trapped her into a criminal's cage.

JAGDEEP. How?

YAMRAJ. By getting everybody's sympathy.

JAGDEEP (*eagerly*). That means I *got* sympathy?

YAMRAJ. You are dead to the world, yet cling to your previous life.

JAGDEEP. Savita must be drowning in grief.

YAMRAJ. This is a conspiracy.

JAGDEEP. You call love a conspiracy!

YAMRAJ. What else, when there is no pleasure like seeing your lover pine for you in your absence.

JAGDEEP (*snapping his fingers*). Now she'll know. She'll realize my true value.

YAMRAJ (*snapping his fingers*). You cannot snap fingers here. It's banned.

JAGDEEP. Bechari, what all she has to bear! Tears in her eyes, hair undone, her bindi wiped out, she must be wearing a tattered black sari and crying her heart out.

YAMRAJ. Do you want to see what she is doing now?

JAGDEEP. I won't be able to bear her pain.

YAMRAJ. Then let it be.

JAGDEEP. No, no. I'm willing to put up with anything for love.

YAMRAJ. Decide.

JAGDEEP. I said Yes. Show me!

YAMRAJ. Look here then.

Darkness.

SCENE 4

RANCHOD's *house. Afternoon.* SAVITA *and* SHARMISHTHA *are arranging Kashimiri curtains, both are dressed in touristy clothes.*

SHARMISHTHA. This looks like the real Kashmir now.

SAVITA (*singing*). I wanted to roam the mountains without help/

I wanted to behold every nook and corner of the forests/I wanted to see the valleys and the caves/I wanted to wipe the eyes of weeping rivulets ...

SHARMISHTHA. I'm trembling in the wind.

SAVITA. This must be what they call ice cold winds, winds that melt your bones.

SHARMISHTHA. It has started snowing.

SAVITA. It's three in the afternoon and so dark?

SHARMISHTHA. It'll be difficult to go to Pahalgaon today.

SAVITA. We'll stay here for the next two, three days.

SHARMISHTHA. After that we'll go to Pahalgaon. I'm very keen to go to Pahalgaon.

SAVITA. My teeth are chattering.

SHARMISHTHA. Has Manilal worn a warm coat?

SAVITA. He refused to take a muffler.

SHARMISHTHA. If we hadn't fallen in love with Manilal who would've taken us to Kashmir?

SAVITA. Come in, Manilal.

MANILAL *enters. Wearing outdoor clothes.*

MANILAL (*sings*). Twinkle twinkle little star/How I wonder what you are/Up above the world so high/Like a diamond in the sky.

SHARMISHTHA. It is a lovely poem, isn't it? What does it mean?

MANILAL. The whistling wind has wound the earth around it.

Dark clouds have hidden the sun and established their supremacy. Rain pitter patters on a sheet of ice ... and I am courting two women with my poetry.

Darkness.

SCENE 5

Hell.

JAGDEEP. Savita has forgotten me completely.

YAMRAJ (*imitating him*). Tears in her eyes ... hair undone ... in a tattered black sari ...

JAGDEEP. It would've been better not to have committed suicide.

YAMRAJ. Who invited you to do it? Why didn't you heed Ranchodbhai's advice?

JAGDEEP. How would that old man understand young love, I thought.

YAMRAJ. Nobody cares about sensible advice.

JAGDEEP. What will happen now?

YAMRAJ. Bhagwan, I'm confused.

Lord VISHNU *enters in traditional dress as seen in calendars.*

VISHNU. Why, what is it?

YAMRAJ. This Jagdeep! He committed suicide and is here before his time.

VISHNU. Human beings! They make things difficult for us. Throw him into hell.

YAMRAJ. Hell, ghosts ... there's no space here even to make a promise.

VISHNU. Then throw him out. Let him hang suspended like Trishanku.

JAGDEEP. There is no place in Heaven?

YAMRAJ. No. Chitragupta says that he had forty years left on Earth.

VISHNU. The reason for committing suicide?

YAMRAJ. Love of Savita.

VISHNU. Listen, that guy hanging upside down over a fire, there's some place beside him.

YAMRAJ. The heat will bother him.

VISHNU. Let him suffer. Come Yamraj, let's go back to our game.

YAMRAJ. Forgive me, Lord. On Earth, the Narmada is in spate. Thousands have died. I have a lot of work. I'm very busy.

VISHNU. That means you won't play with me.

YAMRAJ. We had a game yesterday.

VISHNU. You are obsessed with work. Who should I play with now?

JAGDEEP. I can play with you.

YAMRAJ. Then can I leave?

JAGDEEP. Yes.

YAMRAJ *leaves.*

VISHNU. How can you play with me? You are consigned to Hell. And there are no games in Hell.

JAGDEEP. I did not have any faith in God, Geetapaath, the whiplash of Akha's poetry, Mira bhajans ... I haven't done any of it. I cheated in the Geography exams. Is that why you're flinging me into Hell?

VISHNU. Fool! You don't go to Heaven by singing bhajans. Corrupt leaders, smugglers ... arrey, so many artists have gone to Heaven!

JAGDEEP. Then what about natural justice?

VISHNU. Have you seen justice in Nature? Has an honest man's farm ever received rain? Have a dishonest man's crops ever been destroyed?

JAGDEEP. Then what is the Truth?

VISHNU. We accommodate the dead wherever there is place.

JAGDEEP. And if fifteen persons die at the same time?

VISHNU. What are these dice for? We throw dice and decide ... Heaven or Hell!

JAGDEEP. That means there's uncertainty here too ... just like on Earth. What's the difference then?

VISHNU. The difference is that here you can see the dice.

JAGDEEP. Then give me one chance Bhagwan, let me play one round with you.

VISHNU. But this is Hell.

JAGDEEP. Prabhu! How can it be Hell? You are here.

VISHNU. Quick wit!

JAGDEEP. One is coloured by the company one keeps!

VISHNU. What do you have that I don't?

JAGDEEP. Why?

VISHNU. To put at stake.

JAGDEEP. My love for Savita.

VISHNU. And what do you propose I do with it?

JAGDEEP. You have to decide that. I don't have anything else.

VISHNU. Accepted. Let's play.

JAGDEEP. Who'll throw the first dice?

VISHNU. The one who gets the highest number.

JAGDEEP. My turn. Twelve!

VISHNU. Five!

JAGDEEP. There, I have done it.

VISHNU. I want six.

JAGDEEP. You have got only four.

VISHNU. It is trapped in the house.

JAGDEEP. Eight! I've won! Prabhu! I have won!

VISHNU. Ask. What do you want?

JAGDEEP. Savita's love.

VISHNU. That's impossible? You are a dead man.

JAGDEEP. That's upto you.

VISHNU. You are aware, aren't you, that you're in Hell?

JAGDEEP. You're aware, aren't you, that you have lost?

VISHNU. You are in Hell!

JAGDEEP (*loudly*). You have lost.

VISHNU (*loudly*). You are in Hell!

JAGDEEP. I have won this game!

VISHNU. That's right. So be it. You will get Savita's love.

JAGDEEP. Thank you.

Darkness.

SCENE 6

SAVITA's *house. Afternoon. The Kashmiri curtain is lying somewhere in the corner.* MANILAL *enters.* SAVITA-SHARMISHTHA *perform aarti for* MANILAL.

SAVITA. Manilal.

MANILAL. Savita.

SAVITA. Good news.

MANILAL. I know.

SAVITA. That's not possible! If you do, then tell me!

MANILAL. We can rehearse the trip to Kashmir for another month!

SHARMISHTHA. Why?

MANILAL. The white Ambassador won't be delivered this month too.

SHARMISHTHA. When will it be delivered then?

MANILAL. Next month.

SAVITA (*to* MANILAL). This isn't my good news.

MANILAL. I know. You're expecting a guest.

SAVITA. But how did you know?

MANILAL. Ranchodbhai told me.

SAVITA. But how did he know?

MANILAL. He said we should decide the name and size together.

SAVITA. Name is all right, but size?

MANILAL. Godrej 165 litres. Ranchodbhai said that the ice in Kashmir should be real. He has given the deposit, it'll be delivered in a month.

SAVITA. My good news will take full nine months.

SHARMISHTHA. You're going to become a father.

MANILAL. Father. Good. I've never played with a child. How does one play with a child?

NAVNEET *is at the window spying on* SHARMISHTHA.

SHARMISHTHA. Savita is really going to be a mother.

MANILAL. Is anybody there?

SHARMISHTHA. The maid at your service.

MANILAL. Who brought me news of the child?

SHARMISHTHA. Your humble servant.

MANILAL. Ask, ask. And I'll give you whatever you want!

SHARMISHTHA. Really?

MANILAL. Tell me, what do you want? A pearl necklace, a packet of diamonds or an Ambassador car?

SHARMISHTHA. I also want your child.

SAVITA. Sharmishtha wants to be at par with me in everything now.

MANILAL. My love, I'll give you a shining new, perfectly formed child too. Happy?

NAVNEET *enters.*

NAVNEET (*screaming*). No! Don't you dare touch my wife!

MANILAL. I don't know the art of giving her a child without touching her.

SHARMISHTHA. Let him rave and rant, you can touch me.

NAVNEET. Come home!

SHARMISHTHA. I want a child!

NAVNEET. Come home! Now!

SHARMISHTHA. I want a child. Right now.

NAVNEET. How can I get one right away?

NAVNEET *takes* SHARMISHTHA *away.*

SAVITA. Manilal!

MANILAL. Yes?

SAVITA. I want to eat something sour!

MANILAL. I don't believe it.

SAVITA. I want something sour!

MANILAL. Why? Do you want to puke?

RANCHOD *enters.*

SAVITA. Oh! You're back early?

MANILAL. Good. I hardly get to meet you these days.

RANCHOD. How are you Manilal? You haven't left for Kashmir as yet?

SAVITA. We can't go to Kashmir.

RANCHOD. Why?

SAVITA. There's some good news.

RANCHOD. Even before the Kashmir trip?

SAVITA. It's not good to travel to Kashmir in this condition.

MANILAL. There's good news for you.

SAVITA. We are going to have a visitor.

MANILAL. Ranchodbhai, fate has smiled on you.

RANCHOD. It's all by the grace of God.

SAVITA. Better late than never.

MANILAL. Ranchodbhai, for the first time in my life, I envy you.

RANCHOD. You envy me?

MANILAL. Yes, when are you going to celebrate?

RANCHOD. Whenever Savita makes the sweets.

MANILAL. Savita, no more physical stress for you.

RANCHOD. Physical stress? In making sweets?

SAVITA. The person who does it knows. We'll need at least fifteen kilos if they are to be distributed all over the lane.

MANILAL. But why should the entire lane enter into this?

SAVITA. A happy occasion. After so many years. We shouldn't forget the people of this lane. We'll have to give one and half kilos to Vimlaben alone. Lots of people in that house.

RANCHOD. When they got a fridge they gave us only cold water.

SAVITA. Manilal, you tell him. I feel shy.

RANCHOD. What is it Manilal?

MANILAL. Ranchodbhai, you're going to become a father.

RANCHOD *is speechless for a moment.*

RANCHOD. Hari, Hari! Your will prevails.

Darkness.

SCENE 7

Hell. Seeing Scene Six JAGDEEP*'s eyes fill with tears.*

JAGDEEP. Lekin ek baat hai, Bhagwan! I asked for Savita's love today. But never at the cost of Ranchoduncle's happiness!

VISHNU. How does Ranchodbhai come into the picture?

JAGDEEP. The one person who said to me Life is invaluable, don't waste it. He's the one who advised me to take up photography. I'll not be able to bear his unhappiness even if I've to play another round of dice with you.

VISHNU. I will play a game of dice for Ranchodbhai's happiness on one condition.

JAGDEEP. What?

VISHNU. You speak in Gujarati.

JAGDEEP. Fine, Bhagwan.

VISHNU. Throw the dice.

JAGDEEP. Twelve ... Twelve ... Twelve ... Bhagwan, why did my mother die?

VISHNU. Shut up and throw the dice.

JAGDEEP. Twelve ... Twelve ... Twelve ...

Darkness.

SCENE 8

NAVNEET*'s house.* NAVNEET *lies on the cot wearing a vest and dhoti.* RANCHOD *comes by to look him up.*

RANCHOD. How are you today?

NAVNEET. Better.

RANCHOD. You have fallen ill after a long time.

NAVNEET. Yes, I used to get fever very often in school. And you would take care of me.

RANCHOD. In the Sixth standard, you got typhoid ...

NAVNEET. And you took care of me. The good old days!

RANCHOD. Yes, we've crossed many paths together.

NAVNEET. What is the meaning of life?

RANCHOD. Go through life with detachment and faith in God.

NAVNEET. You don't remember anything of the past?

RANCHOD. Did I say that? Sometimes when I see you I lose myself in memories ... the fun and mischief. And I feel like holding your hand and saying Come, let's leave everything and go.

NAVNEET. Come, let's go.

RANCHOD. Ishwar is so kind. He reveals different facets of life through Savita.

NAVNEET. What if there's no God?

RANCHOD. How did the Universe come into being? Who created it?

NAVNEET. It's all for His own pleasure.

RANCHOD. The transformation of unhappiness into happiness.

NAVNEET. What if there's no justice in Heaven and Hell?

RANCHOD. How?

NAVNEET. Suppose you go to Hell, and Manilal to Heaven?

RANCHOD. You are treated according to the sins of your previous births.

NAVNEET. I believe that when a man dies he's reduced to ashes. Nothing remains ...

RANCHOD. What of the soul then?

NAVNEET. Is there a soul?

RANCHOD. The soul leaves the body in the last hiccup of life. After that the ants, insects, vultures ... all know that the soul has left. Then there's no harm in eating the body. It is possible that our time will come tomorrow.

NAVNEET. If you go away, and I leave, what will become of our love?

RANCHOD. I don't have an answer to this question. How do you feel now?

NAVNEET. I had a dream last night.

RANCHOD. What did you dream?

NAVNEET. I can't talk about it. I feel shy.

RANCHOD. Of me?

NAVNEET. Yes. I feel shy of everybody. Shut your eyes and I'll tell you.

RANCHOD. There, I've shut my eyes.

The light dims. NAVNEET *wears* SHARMISHTHA's *sari over his clothes.* RANCHOD *looks on with interest.*

NAVNEET. In the dream it is two in the afternoon. It's dark.

RANCHOD. Dark in the afternoon?

NAVNEET. It's time for Manilal to arrive. I want to set a foolproof trap for him. I've sent Sharmishtha away. I bunk office in the afternoon and get ready to welcome Manilal.

RANCHOD. Cover your head, or he'll recognize you.

NAVNEET. You are cheating. I told you not to see?

RANCHOD. Wear the pleats properly.

NAVNEET. The pallu is visible isn't it?

RANCHOD. Yes. Then what happened?

NAVNEET. Now don't open your eyes. Then I hide a knife in the blouse.

RANCHOD. Be careful.

NAVNEET. Today is the day of reckoning. Either Mania lives or I do. I hide in the darkness ... so that nobody can see me ... and the scoundrel enters.

He is done with wearing the sari. Light fades. SHARMISHTHA *enters.*

SHARMISHTHA. Who? Who is it? A thief has stolen into the house with a knife. Help, help.

NAVNEET. Quiet. Be silent.

SHARMISHTHA. Who is it? Come out!

NAVNEET. This is my house. You get out!

SHARMISHTHA. Never. I own this house.

NAVNEET. It's me, Navneet.

SHARMISHTHA. Why are you dressed up like this?

NAVNEET. Quiet!

SHARMISHTHA. What's going on?

NAVNEET. I'm playing House.

SHARMISHTHA. Wearing women's clothes?

NAVNEET. I wanted to check whether it suits me or not.

SHARMISHTHA. From tomorrow I'll wear the dhoti and vest at home.

NAVNEET. Don't do that. This is the first time I've worn these clothes.

SHARMISHTHA. Even today I wouldn't have known. I came home early and caught you. Oh ma! You have crumpled my new sari.

NAVNEET. I'll get you a new one.

SHARMISHTHA. I'll tell Savita. Come and see what my husband is wearing!

NAVNEET. Don't tell Savita! I'll get you a chiffon sari, a dish-holder, a stainless steel coffee set, a sunmica table and a plastic bucket, but don't even whisper this to Savita.

SHARMISHTHA. Will you get me sauce?

NAVNEET. We can't afford sauce.

SHARMISHTHA (*calls out*). Savita!

NAVNEET. She'll tell Ranchod!

SHARMISHTHA. You tell Ranchodbhai if anyone as much as farts here, so why be ashamed about this?

RANCHOD *laughs.*

SHARMISHTHA. I'll sink into the earth.

SHARMISHTHA *lies on the cot.*

NAVNEET (*to* RANCHOD). Well, the clock strikes three. I hide in the dark. Nobody can see me. I can see the rascal.

Light fades some more. MANILAL *enters in Krishna's apparel. He has a flute in his hand.*

MANILAL (*to* NAVNEET). Priye, it's good that Navneet is not here! Let him disappear forever. Then it'll be just the two of us! See how thoughtful you've been of my arrival? An open door. The dim light of the lamp, low music and you lying there like a yakshagani, inviting me.

NAVNEET (*to* RANCHOD). He appears in *my* dreams and curses me.

MANILAL (*to* NAVNEET). My heart is storming towards you like a river in spate.

NAVNEET (*to* MANILAL). Don't you dare touch her! Recall your god for a minute. That's all you have.

Everybody is stunned.

NAVNEET (*to* RANCHOD). When I saw him I realized. He had worn Krishna's dress. How can Sharmishtha like somebody who dresses like this?

MANILAL (*to* NAVNEET, *in control*). You're the mere cause.

NAVNEET (*to* MANILAL). This pointed knife will pierce your heart right through, and from it will flow warm blood that will cast this floor in red!

NAVNEET *lifts his hand to kill* MANILAL. MANILAL *makes a sign.* NAVNEET'*s hand freezes.*

MANILAL (*peacefully*). Paritranaya sadhunam vinashaya cha dushkrutam ...

NAVNEET (*to* RANCHOD). My hand froze. (*To* MANILAL.) Who are you?

MANILAL. I'm Krishna Kanhaiyya.

NAVNEET. Blasted rascal!

MANILAL *plays the flute.*

NAVNEET. This is a song from the Hindi film *Hero.* Even Ranchod knows that. You should be whipped.

RANCHOD (*to* NAVNEET). You told him this to his face?

NAVNEET. Yes, what else!

RANCHOD (*to* NAVNEET). I don't know that song. How does it go?

MANILAL *plays the flute again.*

RANCHOD. I've heard it somewhere. But I can't remember.

MANILAL (*to* NAVNEET). Why are you so angry with me?

NAVNEET (*to* MANILAL). You arrested my hand to trap my wife and now you're shameless enough to ask me why I'm angry with you?

MANILAL. Sharmishtha gave me her heart on her own. I didn't refuse it. If you want to be angry, be angry with her.

NAVNEET. My hand has gone numb.

MANILAL. Will you lift your hand again?

NAVNEET. No.

MANILAL (*gestures*). Unfreeze.

NAVNEET's *hand unfreezes. He moves his hand backwards and forwards to check its movements.*

NAVNEET (*to* RANCHOD). I lied.

RANCHOD. Hari. Hari. Your will prevails.

Seizing the opportunity NAVNEET *attacks* MANILAL *who gestures again.* NAVNEET *freezes once again in an aggressive pose, like a statue.*

MANILAL (*to* NAVNEET, *as though explaining to a child*). Sharmishtha and Savita have the hearts of gopis. They will run after Krishna. Throw away your anger.

MANILAL *leaves.* NAVNEET *sheds tears of anger in his aggressive pose.* RANCHOD *gets up and strokes* NAVNEET's *head. With this touch,* NAVNEET *is conscious. The light changes.*

RANCHOD *sits next to* SHARMISHTHA *who lies on the cot.* NAVNEET *puts his head on* RANCHOD*'s lap and sobs uncontrollably.*

RANCHOD. Navneet, Navneet, don't cry. Calm down. You burst into tears for something like this? Now you are behaving the way you did as a child. Wipe your tears bhai, calm down. (*Chants.*) Then the dark god said, I remember you/How can I forget the love of childhood/We stayed together for two months, I remember you/How can I forget Sandipani Rishi's house/We slept together/We shared happy and unhappy moments ... You are lucky.

NAVNEET's *sobs subside.*

NAVNEET. Lucky?

RANCHOD. Yes. You have received the knowledge of the Universe.

NAVNEET. I don't know anything.

RANCHOD. In half an hour you have known all the secrets of the world.

NAVNEET. Me? Really?

RANCHOD. My Murari is so naughty. He appeared in Navneet's dream to give me a message. Navneet, I can see the way ahead clearly!

NAVNEET. I can't see anything.

RANCHOD. You're with me, aren't you?

NAVNEET. Always.

RANCHOD. Then come with me.

NAVNEET. Where?

RANCHOD. On the course of action we'll take.

NAVNEET. So, what am I to do?

RANCHOD *whispers into* NAVNEET's *ear.* NAVNEET *listens with astonishment and eager restlessness. Finally,* NAVNEET *agrees.*

Darkness.

SCENE 9

SHARMISHTHA's *house. Afternoon.* RANCHOD *is seated.* MANILAL *enters in ordinary clothes, humming a song.*

RANCHOD. Very happy today?

MANILAL. I live for the happiness of my body. I have no worries about this, neither do I desire to see God.

RANCHOD. If that is the case, can I ask you a question?

MANILAL. Ask. Not one, but many.

RANCHOD. It is a bit private.

MANILAL. I have also dipped into your private life, haven't I?

RANCHOD. You've never asked me about my private matters.

MANILAL. I've no curiosity either. What's the point in making somebody's private life public?

RANCHOD. You know my nature.

MANILAL. That's why I come to your house.

RANCHOD. Savita is my one and only wife, right?

MANILAL. Right.

RANCHOD. And I love her, right?

MANILAL. Right.

RANCHOD. Sharmishtha is Navneet's other half, right?

MANILAL. Right.

RANCHOD. You snatched the love of the two women from our lives. Right?

MANILAL. No. I gave them love. Women are waterfalls of love. Drink as much as you can.

RANCHOD. Savita has made kadhi and daal for you. Sharmishtha has made chevda with puffed rice for you.

MANILAL. Each one has a different notion of happiness.

RANCHOD. Navneet had a dream.

MANILAL. I dwell in dreams.

RANCHOD. He saw you in his dream.

MANILAL. He cannot see anybody but me.

RANCHOD. You froze his hand in the dream.

MANILAL. Froze? He must have lifted it.

RANCHOD. It was you, Krishna!

MANILAL. Me? That too as Murari? You are making a mistake, Ranchodbhai!

RANCHOD. Why?

MANILAL. Because a man who lives with all five elements alert cannot be God.

RANCHOD (*angrily*). Param Prabhu, you will bring light into deep darkness ... You explained the secret of life to him, right?

MANILAL. What are you talking about, Ranchodbhai?

RANCHOD. Can I ask you something?

MANILAL. No, don't ask me, talk to me.

RANCHOD. Who loves Savita and Sharmishtha?

MANILAL. I do.

RANCHOD. Who knows this?

MANILAL. The two of us.

RANCHOD. Should this fact remain restricted?

MANILAL. Yes, it should remain between two families.

RANCHOD. Why?

MANILAL. It is a family matter.

RANCHOD. Are you afraid?

MANILAL. Me?

RANCHOD. Yes.

MANILAL. Why?

RANCHOD. You want to bury love in the house?

MANILAL. You can't build an edifice of love.

RANCHOD. True love should burst like crackers.

MANILAL. What are you saying?

RANCHOD. So you've turned out to be a coward, right?

MANILAL. Worldly wise.

RANCHOD. No, kayar, darpok, bihad. Coward, weak, spineless!

MANILAL. Cultured.

RANCHOD. Declare your love.

MANILAL. Me?

RANCHOD. I have dedicated my wife to Krishna. You accept her.

MANILAL. How?

RANCHOD. Did you ask when you made love to her?

MANILAL. Love just happened.

RANCHOD. It should be made public.

MANILAL. Should I print photographs in the newspaper?

RANCHOD. I didn't think you were childish.

MANILAL. Should I invite the community for a feast?

RANCHOD. It is important that the community knows.

MANILAL. Think of your situation at least.

RANCHOD. *I* will worry about that.

MANILAL. Is it necessary for you to think of everybody?

RANCHOD. Not everybody. Just loved ones.

MANILAL. Leave that to me.

RANCHOD. I had left it to you. I didn't know that you would hide in the house like a frightened rabbit.

MANILAL. Ranchodbhai, I have no need to hide.

RANCHOD. Manilal, I have no need to hide too!

MANILAL. You'll do what you want to, won't you?

RANCHOD. If you cooperate with me.

They are quiet for a second.

Darkness.

SCENE 10

SAVITA's *house.* NAVNEET, RANCHOD *and* SHARMISHTHA *are chanting.*

SHARMISHTHA. Red and gold.

NAVNEET. Yellow and silver.

SHARMISHTHA. Red and gold.

NAVNEET. Yellow and silver.

RANCHOD. Is the colour of an invitation more important than its contents?

NAVNEET. Colour.

RANCHOD. Navneet!

NAVNEET. Gold will not do.

RANCHOD. Then we'll keep it gold and yellow. Happy?

SHARMISHTHA. Yes.

NAVNEET. Will do.

RANCHOD. Write. Ra, Ra, Shriman, Shrimati.

SHARMISHTHA. What is Ra, Ra?

NAVNEET. Go, make some tea.

RANCHOD. Ra, Ra. Rajmaan, Rajaswi, Shriman, Shrimati. We are pleased to inform you that with the blessings of our elders, we have chosen the first day Chaitra for a display of nursery rhyme courtship.

NAVNEET. How do you spell "chosen"? With an "e" or "a"?

RANCHOD. A.

NAVNEET. Go ahead.

RANCHOD. This auspicious event will begin at four pm Mumbai Standard Time. We extend a warm invitation to every husband and wife in your community to remain present.

SHARMISHTHA. Should I write about the ice cream?

NAVNEET. Is the tea done?

SHARMISHTHA. Can't I even remind you?

RANCHOD. At five thirty we will serve kaju-draksh ice cream.

NAVNEET (*to* SHARMISHTHA). Happy?

SHARMISHTHA. Happy.

RANCHOD. The artists of nursery rhyme courtship will be Savita Ranchodlal and Maujila Manilal. Every couple should ...

SAVITA *and* MANILAL *enter hand-in-hand.*

RANCHOD. Here come the English love artists!

SHARMISHTHA. How are the rehearsals going?

NAVNEET. When can we see them?

MANILAL (*to* NAVNEET). You are the producer. You should not interfere in the creative process.

RANCHOD. But tell us what point it has reached.

SHARMISHTHA. So that we know what to write in the invitation card.

VISHNU *enters.*

MANILAL. Who's this?

SAVITA. Who knows?

MANILAL. How did you come here?

SAVITA. Isn't he sweet? Whose child is he? Look at his dress! Did you have a fancy dress competition in school?

RANCHOD. Don't confuse him with all your questions. He looks lost.

SHARMISHTHA. Poor thing. His mother must be hiccuping.

NAVNEET. As though his father wouldn't be bothered at all!

SHARMISHTHA. Men's hearts are made of stone.

SAVITA. That is why a woman is called janani, the birth-giver.

RANCHOD. What's your name?

VISHNU. Vishnu.

RANCHOD. Nice name. What's your father's name?

VISHNU. I have no father.

RANCHOD. You mean he is dead?

VISHNU. He does not exist.

NAVNEET. Your surname?

VISHNU. I'm called Vishnu. I have no surname.

SAVITA. Even at this age he knows that he doesn't know his father's name. Becharo!

VISHNU. I am Swayambhu, the Self-created.

SAVITA. Look, son, you're lost.

SHARMISHTHA. It's our responsibility to take you to your parents.

NAVNEET. Where do you live?

VISHNU. In Heaven.

SAVITA. Isn't he innocent?

SHARMISHTHA. He believes he's Vishnu Bhagwan just because he is wearing these clothes.

VISHNU. I *am* Vishnu.

RANCHOD. Don't harass him. Or he will start crying. Come here. Look son, you are lost. Good boys like you are picked up by all kinds of thieves and dacoits. So give us your address and we will take you to your parents.

VISHNU. I have come from Heaven. I am Bhagwan Vishnu himself and have come to take Ranchod to Heaven.

RANCHOD (*excited*). Really? My Murari? Yashodhara's favourite has come!

NAVNEET. Don't go crazy along with this child.

VISHNU. The Pushpak Viman is parked outside.

NAVNEET. Where?

VISHNU. On the terrace.

NAVNEET. I'm not going to climb up the stairs.

RANCHOD (*chants*). Oh, mother of mine, I have not stolen the butter/I swear on you I have not eaten butter. Come, O Lord.

NAVNEET. Where are you off to?

RANCHOD. The Lord himself has come in his Pushpak Viman. And I won't go?

NAVNEET. What's all this? You are truly Vishnu?

RANCHOD. How rude can you all be? Navneet. How can you talk to God like this?

NAVNEET. No namaskar without chamatkar. Prove that you are God.

SHARMISHTHA. If you are really God, turn day into night.

SAVITA. A dark night where nothing is visible.

SHARMISHTHA. A dark forest.

NAVNEET. We want to hear the howl of jackals.

RANCHOD. You want proof from the Lord himself? Narayan! What's going to happen?

VISHNU. Calm down bhakt. I'll show them my powers. Blackout please!

Darkness.

SHARMISHTHA. Nothing is visible.

SAVITA. It's a dark night.

NAVNEET. I can hear the call of wild animals.

RANCHOD. Bhagwan, I have faith. I do not want to test God. Give us day again.

VISHNU. Lights. General lights, please.

Light. JAGDEEP *is standing on the cot in the midst of the gathering.*

EVERYBODY TOGETHER. Jagdeep, you?

SAVITA. You were dead?

JAGDEEP. Yes.

MANILAL. Then how did you come?

JAGDEEP. Just to meet you. I'm going to go back.

SHARMISHTHA. How is it there?

JAGDEEP. What do I say? Very hot.

MANILAL. Where were you?

JAGDEEP. In Hell, they had me standing in front of the fire.

NAVNEET. There's no fan there?

JAGDEEP. Nobody has a fan there.

RANCHOD. God, why are you harassing him?

VISHNU. There's no place up there for those who come before their time.

SAVITA. Jagdeep, tell us about it! Were you spouting dialogues in Hindi there too?

JAGDEEP. Tumhe yaad karta tha.

NAVNEET. Please don't speak in Hindi.

SAVITA. Whom did you meet there?

JAGDEEP. Yamraj.

SHARMISHTHA. What language does Yamraj speak in?

JAGDEEP. Gujarati and English.

SHARMISHTHA. Not Hindi?

JAGDEEP. Hindi unke bas ki baat nahi. He's not capable of it.

RANCHOD (*excited*). Yashoda Nandan, Devaki Nandan, my dark god, my Krishna has actually come in his Pushpak Viman to take me!

VISHNU. Hurry up. If I get late, Lakshmi will not favour us with her gifts. She wants everything at the right time!

RANCHOD. You go ahead God, I'm following you.

JAGDEEP. Just a minute Ranchodbhai! (*To* VISHNU.) Should I tell him?

VISHNU. Yes, yes. Be frank, but be quick!

JAGDEEP. Ranchodbhai, should I tell you the truth? The Viman has come to take you up. But it's not worth it.

RANCHOD. Why?

JAGDEEP. Yamraj and Vishnu throw the dice and decide, Heaven or Hell.

RANCHOD. That's not true!

JAGDEEP. I've been there.

RANCHOD. God! Tell these misguided souls that they get you only if they lead a clean, pure life.

VISHNU. But that is not true.

RANCHOD. I don't understand.

VISHNU. Nothing. I was playing the dice with this Jagdeep.

SHARMISHTHA. God, you gamble?

VISHNU. Timepass.

NAVNEET. Then what happened?

VISHNU. Ranchod's time was up and in his name the figure twelve fell twelve consequent times.

SAVITA. Has this happened before?

VISHNU. Last time it happened was when Tukaram's time was up.

RANCHOD. That means Heaven and Hell are decided over a game of dice?

VISHNU. Why? Do you have any another suggestion?

RANCHOD. What about my devotion?

VISHNU. That was your timepass. This is my timepass.

SAVITA. Ten years' subscription to *Jankalyan*!

VISHNU. That was a waste of money.

RANCHOD. Has anybody sent back the Pushpak Viman that has gone to fetch them?

VISHNU. Oh no! Tukaram didn't wait for anybody, he just took his seat.

RANCHOD. I won't come.

VISHNU. Why? You'll let go of the happiness of Heaven for the temptations of Earth?

RANCHOD. Forgive me God. This is sheer injustice! I took your name all my life. Does it amount to nothing?

VISHNU. Why, but I am giving you Heaven.

RANCHOD. At the turn of a dice!

VISHNU. That's true.

RANCHOD. Then go back with an empty Pushpak Viman today.

VISHNU. You are creating a problem for me.

RANCHOD. Why?

VISHNU. Pushpak Viman cannot go back empty-handed. Lakshmi will be waiting. None of you know her temper.

MANILAL. Is it all right if I come?

VISHNU. It doesn't make any difference to me.

MANILAL. Thank you.

VISHNU. You are welcome.

JAGDEEP. Mera bhi ek araj sun le, Prabhu! One more favour.

VISHNU. In Gujarati!

JAGDEEP. Get a fan installed where I stand.

VISHNU. That would be needless expense. In six months you'll be reborn here, and it is not hot here. Go ahead. Start the Pushpak Viman. Come Manilal!

JAGDEEP (*to* SAVITA). Main aa raha hoon! Tere paas!

VISHNU *pushes* JAGDEEP *and takes him outside.*

SAVITA (*to* SHARMISHTHA). I'll keep his letter carefully. I'll read it out to him when he grows up.

MANILAL *takes leave of* RANCHOD *and* NAVNEET.

MANILAL. Forgive me my wrongdoings.

RANCHOD. No need for all that!

NAVNEET. Obviously you'll be forgiven!

SAVITA-SHARMISHTHA. No, no, no. Don't sacrifice us and go!

SHARMISHTHA. You are not worried about this broken heart. You are taking leave?

MANILAL. My duty is over.

SAVITA. What about the exhibition of nursery rhyme courtship?

SHARMISHTHA. What of the invitation cards?

SAVITA. Who'll increase the knowledge of the community?

SHARMISHTHA. Who'll spread your nursery rhyme love worldwide?

MANILAL (*to the audience*). After I go, this is your duty.

SAVITA. What about our love?

MANILAL. Duty is higher than love.

SHARMISHTHA. Even so, Manilal ...

SAVITA. Before you leave give us the recipe of your nursery rhyme love.

SHARMISHTHA. One last gift ...

MANILAL. Clean one kilo of love in the winnowing tray and empty it in a vessel. Take care to see that there are no pebbles. Add two spoons of Woman's enchanting form. Hang it on a hook for three days. When it ferments add four spoons of happiness, three spoons of devotion, one spoon of elaichi and two tablespoons of attraction. Have this mixture with honey three times a day, and savour the joy of heaven while living on earth.

VISHNU *enters*.

VISHNU. Ei Manilal! Are you coming or should I take Navneet?

NAVNEET *tries to hide himself behind* RANCHOD.

MANILAL. Let's go, Prabhu.

SHARMISHTHA. After you, who'll get me roses?

SAVITA. Who'll get me mogras?

SHARMISHTHA. Without you the garden of love will wither away.

SAVITA. Our eyes will become rivers of tears!

RANCHOD. Savita, don't worry. I'll get mogras for you.

NAVNEET. Sharmishtha, I'll get roses for you everyday.

MANILAL *and* VISHNU *leave.*

RANCHOD-SAVITA, NAVNEET-SHARMISHTHA *pose as though for a group photograph.*

The light fades, it gets dark slowly.

"Mojila Manilal" was first published in *Gadyaparva* in May 1992.

Bhupen Khakhar, the son of a cloth merchant and a schoolteacher, was born in Bombay. His works have always borne the stamp of his unique personality. Influence is a four-letter word for this iconoclast who came from the chawls of Bombay to storm the bastions of the oh-so-propah Indian art and went on to win the Padma Shri. In his own eyes, though, Khakhar does not think of himself as a particularly rebellious artist. His world is the very real one peopled by men and women whose only topic of conversation may be the dinner menu of the house next door and the rumour mongering rampant in any middle class locality.

After graduating in Economics and Commerce from the Wilson College, Khakhar joined a firm of Chartered Accountants. But in 1961, he announced his intention to be "a painter" and, in the face of great familial opposition, he gave up his job and left Bombay for Baroda to enroll in a master's course in Criticism at the Faculty of Fine Arts. Working part-time as an accountant, he started painting in earnest. This was also when his stories began to appear in Gujarati journals. Today, he still lives in Baroda, and his paintings sell for a fortune each.

Ganesh Devy is an activist working with denotified tribals and has written several articles on mainstream and tribal literature, culture and languages and on Oral Traditions. He has held many distinguished fellowships including The Commonwealth Academic Staff Fellowship and the Fulbright Fellowship. He translates from Gujarati and Marathi into English and has received the Katha Award for Translation. He has also received the Sahitya Akademi Award for his book, *After Amnesia: Change in Literary Criticism.*

Naushil Mehta, a graduate in Chemistry, is a successful playwright and a writer of short fiction. He has also directed a number of plays.

Bina Srinivasan is a writer and a researcher whose writing emphasizes issues concerning women and environment. She is at present working on a comprehensive biography on Bhupen Khakhar's life and work.

BE A FRIEND OF KATHA!

If you feel strongly about Indian literature, you belong with us! KathaNet, an invaluable network of our friends, is the mainstay of all our translation-related activities. We are happy to invite you to join this ever-widening circle of translation activists. Katha, with limited financial resources, is propped up by the unqualified enthusiasm and the indispensable support of nearly 5000 dedicated women and men.

We are constantly on the lookout for people who can spare the time to find stories for us, and to translate them. Katha has been able to access mainly the literature of the major Indian languages. Our efforts to locate resource people who could make the lesser-known literatures available to us have not yielded satisfactory results. We are specially eager to find Friends who could introduce us to Bhojpuri, Dogri, Kashmiri, Maithili, Manipuri, Nepali, Rajasthani and Sindhi fiction.

Do write to us with details about yourself, your language skills, the ways in which you can help us, and any material that you already have and feel might be publishable under a Katha programme. All this would be a labour of love, of course! But we do offer a discount of 20% on all our publications to Friends of Katha.

Write to us at –
Katha
A-3 Sarvodaya Enclave
Sri Aurobindo Marg
New Delhi 110 017

Call us at: 652-4350, 652-4511
or E-mail us at: katha@vsnl.com